STICKLE ISLAND *a novel*

TIM ORCHARD

un

The Unnamed Press
Los Angeles, CA

The Unnamed Press
P.O. Box 411272
Los Angeles, CA 90041

Published in North America by The Unnamed Press.

1 3 5 7 9 10 8 6 4 2

ISBN: 978-1-944700-52-2

Library of Congress Control Number: 2017962795

This book is distributed by Publishers Group West

Cover design & typeset by Jaya Nicely
Cover Artwork by Alexander Vidal

For Elma

With many thanks to: Danielle Svetcov, for her trust in me; Chris and Olivia, for all their work; Wylie O'Sullivan, for her editing skills; and Lee de Montagnac, for opinions and help over the years.

The World is an uncertain place. Best not to have too many fixed ideas.

—Hugh Farrell

STICKLE ISLAND

1

It was 1980 and Margaret Thatcher was attempting to turn the ship of state around by making massive cuts in social services. To those ends a representative from Kent County Council came over to Stickle Island, and a meeting was held in the church, to which the whole island had been invited. Most came. The blow-ins and the locals, including the island's two farmers, John Newman and Henry Stick. The vicar, Julian Crabbe, had never in his five-year sinecure seen his church so full and wondered briefly what it would be like to live in a truly Christian country.

The councillor had come to tell the residents that the grant for the ferry to the mainland was to be cut. Although there was still one working fishing boat, the ferry was the island's lifeline. It took the children to school and the farmers' produce to market, and brought the dole money to the post office.

Kent County Council, like most others, had been placed under strict financial restrictions, and the councillor explained reasonably, as politicians do, that the islanders were going to be screwed and there was nothing they could do about it. They weren't alone; cuts were pretty much across the board and anything that could be was to be sold to the private sector. In fact the ferry was already privately owned but had survived since the 1950s only by dint of the council grant. He made it plain: if the islanders wished to stay on Stickle, they must fund the ferry themselves. Otherwise, they should move to the mainland.

Like most people, the Stickle Islanders took things for granted; they did not expect drastic change and weren't ready for it when it came. They received this disastrous news in a kind of stunned silence. It affected every single person there directly and dramatically, and the sudden shock was momentarily too much to take in. They looked around at one another and screwed their faces up in question. They were not a cohesive group. They hadn't come prepared. They weren't organized. A few put up their hands and then, like children, took them down again, realizing they didn't quite know what question to ask.

The first to stand up was one of the farmers, John Newman. An easygoing man in his fifties, John just wanted the facts. "Exactly how much is the grant to the ferry?"

The councillor murmured, cleared his throat, flipped through his papers. He knew it was £35,000 a year—not a huge amount, but it went against convention to talk in real terms about council funds. So instead he talked of the council's need to balance the books and of how cuts were countywide and they were not a special case. He smiled all the while and held up his hands as though he had nothing to do with anything. Responsibility wasn't his. Cuts were cuts, and what could he do? He was just a cog in the wheel, and if it wasn't him it would be someone else.

When the man had finished speaking, John Newman sighed and shook his head. "You didn't answer my question."

Probably every word the councillor had uttered annoyed someone in the audience, and a general hubbub was growing.

D.C. jumped up and shouted, "Have you ever talked to the guy that owns the ferry?"

The councillor shook his head and stuttered, "Well, er, well..."

D.C., one of the first of the blow-ins to come to the island, eight years earlier, carried on. "Yeh, well, you haven't, but I have. Most of the people here know him. He's been running that ferry for years and his dad before him. He doesn't want to stop, and neither does his son, who works with him now. You won't shut us down that easily. Maybe we'll make a deal with the ferry owner. Maybe we'll start a co-op and run it ourselves." It was a daft idea and he knew it. Most of the island inhabitants were on the dole or a pension, but he didn't let that stop him. He jabbed a finger. "What are you? You come here and want to close down this island because it's no longer convenient. You want to take away people's livelihoods and try to tell us it's all out of your hands, it's the cuts, it's orders from above and all that. What are you, a man that opens the doors to the gas chambers and claims no responsibility because it's orders from above? Only following orders, yeh, do you get me? Come the revolution, we'll put you up against a bus and shoot you!"

D.C. was being ridiculous; everybody knew there wasn't a bus service on the island, but it got people going. A few seconds of confused silence fell over the church before, in fits and starts, the whole assembly got to their feet and began shouting and gesticulating and all for their own reasons, and Julian Crabbe, standing beside the councillor, waved his arms and tried, uselessly, to call for calm.

On one of the front pews, the island's other farmer, Henry Stick—strident, slant-eyed, and ready to strike out in any direction—jumped up, grabbed the council's representative by his lapels, and bellowed, "You can't do this! My family have been living on this island since 1066. We owned this bloody island! I pay my rates! I pay my taxes! I bloody well—"

He raised his fist, but his son, Dick; D.C.; and Police Constable Paloney rushed forward and together grabbed him and wrestled him away down the nave.

Henry Stick's outburst provoked further uproar. People left their seats and crowded forward. Their raised voices rung around the church. The councillor backed off behind the altar, arms held in front of him like a man in a church full of zombies. Julian Crabbe hopped this way and that, begging for moderation without hope of getting it.

Meanwhile, halfway down the nave, Henry Stick pulled D.C.'s hand off his shoulder. "Get off me! It's people like you who've helped ruin this bloody island! Bloody hippies and bloody communists and bloody, bloody drug-taking bloody anarchists! You're all a bunch of freeloading bloody time wasters!"

Henry Stick was a big bull of a man gone to seed and, with a few drinks in him, tended toward easy aggression. From behind his father, Dick, a post-punk left in the New Wave backwash, pleaded with his eyes for D.C. to let it go. The trouble was D.C. couldn't—never had, never would.

"Fuck you. What are you when you're at home then, eh? Lord of the manor? More like king in your own kitchen, if you're lucky," D.C. sneered, sweeping his hair off his face, flaring his nostrils, and sniffing at Henry Stick's mouth. "Been at the cider, have you?"

Tension rippled through Henry Stick, but before he could move, Dick grabbed his shoulders and PC Paloney moved deftly between the two men. "Let's calm down, shall we? I don't want to have to arrest anyone."

PC Paloney was twenty-four, with cheeks so red they looked freshly slapped. When he looked in the mirror in the morning, even he had a job to take himself seriously.

With a smirk, D.C. shook his head and then, almost like a gentleman, stepped back. "And what you going to do with us once you've arrested us? Keep us prisoner in your living room?"

A vision of the police house and the total mess it was in flashed into PC Paloney's mind. He sighed and said, almost hopelessly, "There's no need for cheek. I am the law here."

The two men looked at each other over Paloney's shoulders and both began to grin. Paloney sighed and pulled a face. He'd been on the island for three years and had yet to make an arrest. Despite any personal animosity, when it came to the law, the islanders stuck together. He'd seen it time and time again. It seemed to be the natural order of things and not worth arguing about.

Although there was still a vocal air of resentment, the vicar had managed to calm the islanders down enough for the councillor to explain that the cuts wouldn't come into effect until the following April. April was eleven months away, and when he'd finished speaking, he watched his words sink in and most of their eyes soften as time pushed the urgency of change into the nebulous future.

The councillor loved people—they were mostly gullible idiots—and, confidence regained, he decided to get out while the getting was good. He pushed his way through the islanders' ranks toward the door. At the entrance, Henry Stick stood with his son and Paloney. As he passed, the councillor straightened his tie and squared his shoulders. He had a few words for that lump of a farmer and his 1066 and all that.

With an oily grin, he said, "People like you make me sick. Don't you realize you, this island, means nothing? You're finished! 1066? We at the council couldn't care if you were here with the dinosaurs, the ferry is going to be cut and that's an end to it and to you. It's a foregone conclusion. Attack me if you like, but it won't change a thing!" Then, with a nod back toward D.C., said, "Co-op? You lot couldn't organize a piss up in a brewery!"

He strutted away from the church into the fading May evening, job done. He didn't have to worry about the ferry, for the council had chartered a launch. It was waiting for him at the jetty.

2

Uninhabited and insignificant ever since the dawn of time, Stickle Island wasn't even worth naming for a thousand years. Situated a mile or so off the Kent coast, almost opposite Dymchurch, the island was a little over four miles long and less than a couple of miles wide, and as D.C. said, when he moved there from London in 1972, "You could walk around the whole place in a day." He bought himself a bike.

Stickle's first historical mention was in the Domesday Book (1086), where it was called Stivell Island. The island had been a giveaway, an act of generosity to a minion by a newly enthroned king. After the Battle of Hastings in 1066, William the Conqueror gifted it to his favorite harpist, one Alain Stivell, for penning a charming little ditty about that loser, King Harold, getting an arrow in his eye.

Although from a humble, rural background in the north of France, Alain Stivell wasn't an inbred idiot, and aware of the fickleness of kings, he moved to the island within weeks and never left again. Alain's aim, having been lucky once, was to stay lucky and to be forgotten. This was a family trait that persisted down through the generations. By 1086 Alain had built a modest manor house, and the Domesday Book notes the island to have sixty serfs, fifteen milk cows, a bull, a warren, and numerous sheep. Alain paid his due taxes, sent his quota of men, when asked, for whatever war was current, but he kept his head down. The island produced wool, mutton, milk, and beef, and slowly over time, as the family became anglicized, their name along with that of the island became Stickle.

By the early seventeenth century, like many another country squire of that time, the family's fortunes had sunk so low they were forced firstly to mortgage the original manor house and later to sell some small parcels of the land to stop the banks foreclosing. As Stivell had down the years become Stickle, so with their diminishing fortunes it seemed their name contracted again, until by the late 1670s it had become Stick, the name the few remaining members of that ancient family still go by to this day.

The family fortunes were revived somewhat in the eighteenth century, when the island became a staging post for smugglers running brandy, wine, and lace between France and the Kent coast. They say the Sticks and Dr. Syn (the Scarecrow) were hand in glove for many a year. The contraband was hidden from the revenue men in cellars beneath the old manor house. With the new money, the Sticks flattened the ancient manor house and built a new one, but for obvious reasons the huge cellars beneath the old house remained intact but hidden. At that time more than three hundred people lived on the island, mostly involved in agriculture, fishing, or the more nefarious trades.

Although in most ways the industrial revolution passed the island by, it didn't pass its inhabitants by. The search for a better life began and, with it, the slow drain of the island's population to the mainland. The decline and depopulation continued, hastened at the beginning of the twentieth century by the First World War and the Great Depression of the 1930s. Without sufficient manpower to work it, swaths of the island became, by default, common land.

It was hard times. To keep afloat the Sticks, in the late 1930s, sold over two hundred acres to the Newmans. The Newmans were a hardworking family, mostly interested in milk, with a few sheep on the side. The Sticks didn't dislike the Newmans, but it hurt the proud remains of Alain Stivell's family, small as it now was, to accept the changing times and fortunes. Come the onset of the Second World War, the Stick family owned only the one farm, a few laborers' cottages, and a couple of houses in the village.

Historians say, at the end of the Second World War, the soldiers wanted to come back to a quiet life by home and hearth, but in fact, few came home to Stickle. Once they had seen the world, Stickle didn't match up. It was a backwater. Most of rural Kent was a backwater.

Through the 1950s and early 1960s, places like Dymchurch, St. Mary's Bay, Margate, and plenty of other south coast towns flourished from the boom in family holidays, but Stickle, even with a twice daily ferry from Dymchurch, offered nothing. No trailer parks or campsites, guesthouses or hotels. There wasn't even a pub.

By the late 1960s Stickle had become a bit like one of those islands up in the Hebrides, St. Kilda, or the like, where the population level had shrunk so far as for life on the island to become almost unsupportable, but people lived on anyway, the way they do.

The ferry still came and took the handful of children to school in Dymchurch, the two farms still survived because a milk truck came twice a week to collect the milk, and the farmers took the rest of their produce to wholesalers on the mainland, but the church was empty and the shop/post office hung on by dint of the fact that it was the only shop on the island.

Then, in the early 1970s, the blow-ins (people like D.C.) started to arrive—the alternatives, the ex-hippies on a new route, the embryonic proto-crusties, the organic ne'er-do-wells, the macrobiotic custard-tart eaters—some clutching a copy of John Seymour's *Self-Sufficiency*. But those were the times they were living in, and anyway, they were bringing new life and the island revived a little bit.

D.C. didn't really fit into any of the above but had come to the island for Petal and his Julie, come because he didn't want to lose them. The idea had been Julie's, but then most of the good things that had come to him had come from Julie. It hadn't been easy at first. The pace of life was so slow he'd felt like he was speeding all the time. He'd walked too fast, spoken to quickly, sneered when he could have smiled. He still walked too fast and sneered once in a while, but now Stickle was his home and he had his place in it. The idea of leaving wasn't even an idea.

3

The spring of 1980 was a strange spring. Some analysts maintained the extreme and weird weather patterns over the UK were the onset of the coming new ice age, while others claimed it was the beginning of global warming and we would all soon be living desert style on the periphery of the new Sahara. Then again, to many familiar with the vagaries of the English weather, it was just another dodgy summer. The truth was, even for England, the weather went beyond atrocious.

Yorkshire and the far north were plagued by a drought so severe the reservoirs dried, rivers and lakes became muddy puddles, fish floundered and drowned on air, livestock died of thirst in the fields. Bushfires burned, laying waste to forests and moorland alike. In the cities, factories and businesses closed, and the army was drafted in to distribute water from pump stations and to keep the peace.

In Lincolnshire, through the months of April and May, every kind of frozen water pelted from the sky. It was spring but snow, ready-made into balls, splattered down against everything moving or still. The sleet was like buckshot and the gelid rain was like having a slushy thrown in your face. Then, come June, hailstones the size of penny gobstoppers plummeted to earth at the speed of meteors entering Earth's atmosphere, smashing greenhouses, office windows, and car windscreens, bruising and breaking bones. Ice-cold winds straight from the Ural Mountains came next, freezing the new potatoes in the ground and burning the burgeoning winter wheat into mush. The county was a mess.

In Devon and Cornwall it poured unceasingly. It was biblical. So much rain fell that good Christians threw up their hands and started building mini-arks in their back gardens in an effort to save their pet hamsters, goldfish, pythons, and pit bulls, their rug rats and ankle biters, and their wives. They pleaded to their invisible deity for salvation, but if those feet ever did walk England's green and pleasant land, he was wearing thigh waders. It was a deluge. The floods raged for weeks. Country lanes became unnavigable torrents; major roads a hydroplaning nightmare of mangled metal. Embankments collapsed, carrying away railway tracks, telegraph poles, signal boxes, and all that infrastructure we always take for granted. Rivers burst their banks, and everything from car showrooms and trailer sites to entire small villages was swept down to the sea in great heaps.

In Wiltshire, Hampshire, Oxfordshire, and all those other 'shire-type places—the "stockbroker belt counties" that are almost in the country, where no one from the actual country could afford to live anymore and where life was lived quiet and safe, primped and cleaned by a small army of domestics and gardeners—even those most peaceful of shires weren't exempt from the mayhem of that summer. Dozens of mini-earthquakes rocked and rippled through the glorious south. Down came conservatories, carports, and children's playhouses. It wasn't chaos in the Krakatoa-west-of-Java sense, but it did force several merchant bankers, stock market traders, and advertising executives to take a day or two off to tidy up.

On the other hand Kent, the so-called garden of England, basked through April with just enough rain for the crops. May was as calm and peaceful as it should be in myth and reality and in the Darling Buds of —. And June? The beginning was as beautiful as any living creature could hope for, and Kentish folk watched their TVs and all the strange meteorological happenings up and down the country and smiled at their own good fortune and that of their county. They felt safe and a little smug.

Then the winds came, howling, to Kent. Ten days without respite. Cyclones, mini-tornadoes, hurricanes, whirlwinds, twisters—all tempestuous and violent. Across the county, high-sided vehicles toppled and were blown into piles like giant Jenga blocks. The motorways were closed. Roofs disappeared. Cars were upended. Stables, garages, and anything that wasn't nailed down just blew away. Crops were flattened, ripening fruit ripped from bushes and trees, and like those old-time pictures of First World War battle scenes, whole areas of woodland were torn up and left desolate.

On the coast the devastation was far worse. The ferry ports to the Continent were completely closed. Holiday towns like Margate, Herne Bay, Ramsgate, and Broadstairs were battened-down ghost towns. The roller coaster in Margate's Dreamland was reduced to firewood, and a brace of intrepid anglers on Herne Bay Pier were swept to their death. Nothing particular happened in Ramsgate or Broadstairs, but then nothing ever had. Everywhere else along the coast, fishing boats, yachts, and all forms of small craft were flung onto promenades and beachfronts, smashed willy-nilly to matchwood against harbor walls. Thousands of swanky beach huts were trashed. It was ten days of total mayhem. There were no oysters for sale in Whitstable.

On the eleventh morning the residents of Stickle Island were waking, relieved the battering had finally ceased. They yawned and stretched, and some went back to sleep and some made tea and thought of this or that and some thought about sex and some had sex and some who thought about sex but couldn't have sex masturbated instead, and the truth was, being Stickle, for most people there was nothing much to get up for anyway. And they liked it that way.

Situated in what amounts to the English Channel, Stickle often had bad winters. In winter, wind chill was a real factor, and people had always naturally built low, and most houses were surrounded by high blackthorn hedges or tough stands of stunted oak and ash, which, apart from helping cut out the wind, gave the individual islanders a sense of privacy. A couple of chimneys lost pots, but mostly all was well. It seemed Stickle Islanders had been prepared for a hurricane for close on a thousand years.

And in that empty, early eleventh morning, Si Newman was driving a tractor and trailer along the beach field track. A herd of black-and-white cows was waddling along behind. Si was a big, easygoing guy, the only son of John Newman, one of the island's two farmers. Si had the remains of a bacon sandwich in one hand. At the gate he stuffed the rest of the sandwich into his mouth and jumped down to let the cows into the field, and as he pulled himself back up into the cab, he glanced down the track toward the beach at Fishtail Bay.

At twenty-two years old, Si had the easy animal grace of a latter-day Seth Starkadder. Levi's rolled up to the top of his heavy work boots, a crewneck sweater under a quilted body warmer, and a battered fedora perched on the back of his head, he seemed as he hung there to be posing, but he wasn't, he was just looking. In a way, like the cows, he was merely happy to be out in the world again.

And what a lovely world. Stickle Island at its best. Beautiful now after the storms. Calm and washed clean. The sea a fluid mirror of blue gray lapping gently on the strand. The sun just hovering above the horizon, still pale in a pale cream sky but already casting a beneficent glow over the whole old island.

23

4

Si pulled himself up—one arm on the cab roof, the other on top of the open door—and balanced. Half of his mind was focused on a second breakfast, but something had caught his eye, something on the stretch of beach below the field.

Fishtail Bay almost explained itself. It was a sickle of perfect golden sand set between low, gracefully curving rocky promontories. Here, on this beach, things gathered. In earlier centuries, when need turned to must, Stickle Islanders weren't above a bit of wrecking. In storms they would set lookouts to spy ships in trouble and light fires on the cliffs to lure distressed boats onto the rocks.

Terrible perhaps, and obviously those days, like the days of Dr. Syn and smuggling, were long gone, although something of the spirit remained. Luckily the average man didn't have to kill poor innocent sailors anymore just so his family could live, and anyway, whatever flotsam or jetsam gathered along the tide line these days was mostly rubbish, plastic ducks or shoes already ruined by salt water. Nothing worth murdering anyone for.

Si drove the tractor and trailer along the track until he came to a gap in the dunes, where a wide sandy path cut to the beach. What he'd seen was a dark, almost black brick, getting on for a meter square. It glistened dully in the early-morning light. Once on the beach, Si immediately noticed the three other similar bales, scattered along the high-tide line. He studied the first of the bales. Covered in thick opaque plastic, it was impossible to see the contents. He gave it a shove with his foot. It was heavy.

D.C. had already been on the beach for an hour or more. Fishtail Bay was where he usually collected his firewood, and after a storm was the best time. Today that task had been forgotten. D.C. watched Si from the rocks. Si was like a gift: young, innocent, always ready to lend a helping hand, and, even better, he had a tractor, a trailer, and a barn. D.C. needed all three. Slack tide had been over an hour ago, and the old rising briny would soon take this bounty back into its arms. Sure, he could probably drag them a bit farther up the beach, but D.C. didn't fancy all that wasted effort when there was machinery at hand.

Si strolled along the strand checking each bale, and D.C. followed behind, unnoticed. The fourth bale had a knife cut in its outer covering, and beneath the double skin of heat-sealed plastic was more plastic, then a covering of burlap. Si squatted and peered into the bale, which seemed to be crammed with some kind of vegetable matter. As he made to put his hand through the slash, D.C. tapped him on the shoulder.

Too young for a heart attack, Si jumped and turned, eyes wide, like he'd been caught with a hand in the till. When he saw D.C., he pushed his hands into the pockets of his Levi's like nothing was nothing. "Where did you come from?"

With a friendly sneer, D.C. nodded. "Hardly Robinson Crusoe, are you? Friday would have fucking eaten you by now! I've been here all the time. Didn't you notice my footprints?"

Si looked around on the sand. There were the footprints.

"Anyway you're lucky—I ain't resorted to cannibalism yet. Still got a pig to slaughter come this autumn." D.C. gestured to the bales. "What do you reckon? There's a couple more up on the rocks there."

Si followed the direction of D.C.'s arm, and sure enough there were two more of the bales washed up on the rocky promontory at the far end of the bay.

"Guess what's inside."

Si shrugged. "Don't know, looks like some kind of fodder or something?"

With a shake of his head, D.C. pushed him out of the way. "Fucking farmers! All you think about is feeding or fucking your animals!" Shoving his hand inside the cut bale and drawing out a handful of dark green matter, D.C. held it up to Si's nose. Si sniffed.

It wasn't as though Si didn't recognize the smell or even what he was seeing, because that would have been ridiculous. It was circumstance. At that time, on this bright morning, Si was thinking only of cows and an auxiliary breakfast, and it wasn't until D.C. pulled a joint from the top pocket of his combat jacket that Si truly understood. Waving the joint under Si's nose, D.C. sparked it up and, after a pull, passed it on. "Best Colombian, same as that grass I got a couple of months ago when I was in London, remember?" Si sniffed the spliff and took a tentative pull.

Si's father, John Newman, was one of the very few people D.C. had true respect for. He was the first person on Stickle to sell land or rent cottages to blow-ins, and D.C. had been living on his land ever since he'd arrived with Julie and Petal.

To Si, D.C. had always been like some dodgy uncle. Not dodgy in that wicked what's-that-in-your-pajamas-type thing. No. It was books and ideas, but then again, it was D.C. who'd turned him on at his sixteenth birthday party with a pipeful of excellent hash, but then again, it was also D.C. who always reminded him he'd pulled a whitey. Being sick behind the couch isn't a good move, even if it is in your own home on your birthday.

As for D.C., the fact that he liked Si was irrelevant. He needed the bales moving. It was simple. They represented manna from heaven to him. Born with nothing and brought up in a series of foster homes, he came to adulthood still with nothing, and he'd lived on his wits ever since then, but then, if you'd asked him, he'd say he didn't give a fuck. Not about this or that or any fucking thing. He didn't like the past and didn't trust the future. But he liked moments like this. To D.C., especially on that beach at that time, it was the only time that mattered, and this, *this* was the sort of luck he'd waited his whole life for. A personal, particular time, when the world turns and everything changes. That was what D.C. thought.

What D.C. really needed was Si's help, but when he asked, Si didn't answer. The smoke had hit him and he plonked himself down on the nearest bale and studied the sea. It was hard for D.C. to control himself; he was so excited and was desperate for Si to be excited too. He needed that tractor and trailer. That barn. He spread his arms wide and jerked them about. "Some weird shit gets washed up on this beach! Remember all those plastic ducks?" He took a couple of breaths, looked about, and tried to imagine a brave new world. "But this, this, this is like—it's like... ! This is like finding a gold mine in your back garden! A fucking oil well! Have you got any idea how much this lot is worth?"

Si moved his shoulders; he didn't seem to know and couldn't care. Almost to himself, he said, "Tide's on its way in."

D.C. saw the sea, but he also saw the future and for once in his life it was a bright place. That was a new feeling. It made him happy, silly. He wanted Si's attention. He slapped his thighs, threw his arms out wide again, grabbed Si and, yanking him upright, almost did a little dance. "Si, this is like providence, you know? Like, we'll never have to worry about money ever again! Can you imagine that?" Si was still looking out to sea. Stopping for a moment, D.C. followed his gaze and said, urgently, "You're right, you're right, I'd forgotten! The tide's coming in. Get your tractor and trailer down here, man! You got the one with the forklift on the front?"

Si nodded and took a couple more pulls on the spliff. He was unsure about what he was getting into. He said, "What are we going to do?"

D.C. sighed, came close to Si, and, putting an arm around the younger man's shoulders, drew him in slowly, affectionately, until their heads touched, and then quietly, but not without a modicum of menace, he said, "You've got a bloody great barn up there." Si tried to pull away but D.C. held him. "This is a chance in a lifetime. We'll figure out what to do later, let's just get it all off the beach, for fuck's sake!"

The motorbike didn't exactly shatter a silence, because on the beach that morning was a bunch of those argumentative seagulls caterwauling about this or that, and beneath their raucous cries, various other smaller birds were twittering and chirruping, and then there was the gentle roll and rumble of the sea that never dies, the relentless grind of gravel until it becomes sand. Under that was the softer sound of the breeze rustling the sedges and all, but the noise of the bike's engine coming down to the beach overlaid all and every other sound as though it were silence.

Dick Stick and Petal arrived, skidding to a halt in a shower of sand. Although New Wave was already almost passé, Petal and Dick were as New Wave as Stickle Island had ever had, but then again, in a community as small as Stickle, it wasn't hard to be weird. Dick was punk'd up in skintight black jeans, a leather jacket, and Docs. His hair was green and red and stood up in little gelled spikes, and as the bike slid to a halt, Dick reached up in an almost compulsive gesture and touched the varicolored spikes. Petal didn't have to do anything to look good in her tartan miniskirt, fishnets, leather jacket, and Docs.

At seventeen, Petal knew it all and was already convinced most men were pretty stupid, and she wasn't wrong. Once when she'd asked her dad what he was thinking about as he lay on the couch staring at the ceiling, he'd replied, "Pies." So far in their relationship, she'd never dared to ask Dick what he was thinking.

D.C. gave Dick Stick the evils. It was a dad thing. The way Petal was, wasn't Dick's fault—D.C. knew she was born stroppy and D.C. loved her unconditionally, despite and because of it. So, harshly, he said, "What you two doing here?"

Petal wasn't having any of it. Stepping off the pillion and pointing at her father, she said, "No! It's what do you think *you're* doing here!" Bunches of her pink hair were held at the sides of her head by fluorescent-green Go Go's, and the fluffy bunches waggled when she spoke. Stoned, D.C. and Si began to giggle, and Dick, despite Petal's warning glance, couldn't help a little chortle.

They made her want to stamp her feet in the sand, but she knew, even if she did stamp her feet in the sand, it wouldn't have made any difference, and when she did, they just laughed some more. She said, "Don't patronize me, you. Look at you, two middle-class farmers' sons and my dad!"

Pathetic. Petal believed she had the upper hand on most men because, in literature anyway, a good-looking, clever woman usually did have the upper hand. That was what clever women did. It is what most clever people did.

Stoned as he was, Si had surreptitiously watched Petal from the moment she arrived, but his own feelings for her embarrassed him, and when, as she spoke, she turned her gaze full on him, he didn't know what to do. It felt as though recently something had subtly changed. He didn't know, wasn't sure. Was she looking at him with those eyes? The three of them had been close friends for years. There wasn't much to do on Stickle, but what there was they had done together. Nights sitting in front of the fire in Si's room, stoned, music on, no problem. When Dick and Petal had got together it had seemed natural, despite his own want. Anyway, what could he do? They were his friends. He turned to Dick and, with a wonky grin, gave him a friendly poke on the arm. Dick smiled back and shrugged.

D.C. sighed and started to walk about in tight little circles, chewing his lip. Petal always had it over on him and he knew it and knew that she knew it. It was that unconditional love thing that he couldn't account for, that no one can account for, and it always left him feeling like an idiot. She was precious and probably the best thing about his life, but still, he couldn't let it alone because unconditional love does that to you. Castaneda was right, a child creates a hole in you, but as yet, he'd been unable to repair it. He pointed at her and waggled his finger: "Does your mother know where you are, where you've been? And anyway, why aren't you wearing a crash helmet?" He kicked sand.

When D.C. tried to play the heavy dad it just made Petal want to laugh. She sucked air through her teeth. "Stop it, Dad! Mum knows what I do, and anyway, we only came across the field!"

Regretting it before the words left his mouth, D.C. stopped in front of Petal and said, "You been out all night? Where you been?"

Narrowing her eyes, Petal laughed. "Where have I been? We live on an island, Dad!"

D.C. shook his head. "Don't look at me like that. I am your father, you know!"

With a derisory giggle, Petal said, "Are you? You better talk to Mum about that—you know what you hippies were like with your free love and everything."

D.C. hated it when people called him a hippie. Fuck that! He never was, never had been! Petal could get away with it, but to D.C., being called a hippie was a total insult. He'd never belonged to any creed, religion, movement, social scene, or cult. All he wanted to be was himself. Everything else was decoration: a haircut, a style of jeans, a hat.

A Polish guy he'd met one time had told him, "You can be sure who your mother is but you can never be sure about your father, unless he takes a paternity test." In truth, D.C. didn't care; it went much deeper than the lucky sperm. He tried again, in a softer tone. "All right, all right, but why are you here now?"

With a shrug, Petal nodded toward the nearest bale. "You know, I've learned some things from you, Dad, but the one thing I learned most about is drugs. We're here for the same reason as you."

Holding up his hand like a cop directing traffic, D.C. shook his head. "No way! You must be joking! It's mine and Si's. Finders keepers, right, eh, Si?" He put an arm around the young man's shoulders and plowed on before Si could muster an answer. "Anyway, I was down here while you and Dip Stick there were still in your pit, and possession is nine points of the law."

None of her father's bullshit was new to Petal. She wasn't impressed. "His name is Dick, Dad! You don't possess anything, and as for the law, this is illegal drugs and this is a public beach, *right*! Anyway, we're here now and we were down here last night when this lot was washed up, so so much for your finders keepers."

D.C. didn't want to argue. In fact, combative as he generally was, he didn't know how to argue with Petal. Ever since Julie and he parted ways, it had seemed his relationship with his daughter had been on her terms. He didn't understand exactly why, because he and Julie were still good friends. It was like a teenage-girl thing. Julie had told him, "With girls you ask them questions about the things they are interested in, what they think, their emotions. Be sensitive."

That much he already knew. He'd read the feminist books and lived with the reality. He didn't mind. Everybody has to change up sometimes to stay alive. Guys need to get sensitive. Okay. So D.C. did or at least tried. Sometimes it worked, but sometimes with Petal it all went wrong. Like the time when she was thirteen or so and had come to see him in his trailer in a foul mood. Nothing he did or said was right. He didn't know why. He tiptoed around her for a time, asked her stuff about school and other things he wasn't remotely interested in, tried to divert her attention, and capered about the interior of the trailer, which wasn't easy, but nothing moved her mood.

D.C. thought about all the time he lived with Julie and how he'd noticed her moods and how they went with her menstrual cycle, and he thought about Petal and the age that she was and maybe that was it and maybe now was a good time to be the sensitive father. Let her know he understood. He didn't. What D.C. found out was that thirteen-year-old girls don't really want to talk to their fathers about their period. Petal had stormed out of the trailer. It was six months before she came again. It was one of the worst times of his life.

Even now, four-odd years later, he was still unsure of where the boundaries lay. In all of his dealings with Petal he was afraid she wouldn't see him anymore, wouldn't talk to him anymore, wouldn't, just wouldn't. It was a loss he couldn't bear. So, not knowing what to say, he floundered on: "Down here, while that storm was on? What do you think you were doing? That was dangerous. You could have got washed out to sea and drowned! You could have died! You could have caught pneumonia! Down here! All night!" He sounded stupid to himself, so he stopped speaking.

Petal continued as though he hadn't said a word: "We've got as much right to this as you. You can't just take it, it's not yours." She stopped, thought a quick thought, and went on. "In fact, this stuff here should be for the community, for the people of the island. You know very well what the government wants to do—you were at the meeting when that man came over from the county council. In fact, you were the one who said we were going to start a co-op and make a deal with the ferry owner. What else are you going to do? Sit on the island and smoke this lot while they take away the funding for the ferry? They want to shut this island down and move us all to the mainland, and that means you as well, Dad!" She waved an arm at the bales on the beach. "This could keep Stickle alive. There's plenty. We could do things, change things."

Without a thought, Dick said, "She's right! We could become a collective!" Dick thought green-and-red hair and tight jeans would change the course of humanity. He was the kind of guy who aided the revolution in a radical, nonverbal kind of way by dressing cool. His political ideas were sartorial, and it was true that, to him, Maoist uniforms were cooler than the way the president of America dressed in his suits, and so it followed that collectivism must be better than capitalism, sartorially at least, but then again, he also went with the Dead Kennedys and the fact that a holiday in Cambodia, where everyone dressed in black, was basically negative. And he didn't like the plastic bags over the head—that wasn't a good look. Anyway, the world needed color, end of. He said, again, "Yeh, a collective."

Before D.C. could reach over and strangle him, Petal cut in. "Exactly! Who do you think *you* are? This find should definitely be for the island. Anyway, as you old hippies would say, yeh, power to the people! This is the people's stash. This could alter everything."

The people! D.C. didn't give a fuck about the people, never had. Everybody was the people, and just like him, they would roll over anybody to get their bit. It wasn't the law of the jungle; it was just the law. He wanted to explain but couldn't be bothered, as time was tramping on, and anyway, because he'd started like a prick, he thought he'd finish like one. He pulled faces and made useless threats like some bad-tempered kid and shoved pathetically at the nearest bale. He wasn't even fooling himself.

As a favor, Petal cut him down from the tree before he could hang himself. "Don't even bother, Dad." She turned to Si. "We've just been up to the house, Si, we were going to get you to come down with the tractor and trailer, but your dad told us you were already out with the cows." She let it hang a moment and looked at him. "We could load it up and hide it in your barn."

Too stoned to think, Si couldn't look at Petal because she was too lovely. He turned away and plonked himself down on the bale again and watched the sea. After thirty seconds or so, he stuttered, "W-what about my dad?"

In unison, Dick, Petal, and D.C. said, "What about him?" Then D.C. added, "We'll put the bales down the back of the barn. We'll put a tarp over 'em."

Si didn't like to argue and he didn't want to explain that he didn't care about the grass the way the others seemed to. Si liked a smoke, but he cared about the cows and their hay and silage, about the sheep, about the chickens and collecting the eggs; he cared about the couple of geese he raised for Christmas. And although they argued the way fathers and sons did, he loved his dad and didn't like to deceive him more than necessary. Lifting his chin in Dick's direction, he muttered, "What about your dad's barn?"

Dick hemmed and hawed and blushed and said, hopelessly, "Come on, Si, you know what my dad's like. If he found out about this he'd have us all in jail. That man's got no mercy." Dick knew that wasn't exactly true, but it was an easy out.

Looking over his shoulder at them, Si said, "Look, I don't know. What if Paloney sees us? What if he catches us? That's jail, isn't it?"

D.C. laughed. "He couldn't catch a bloody cold! I'll deal with Paloney. Anyway, Paloney was only sent here to keep an eye on us." He poked himself in the chest with his finger and sneered, "Us poor misbegotten blow-ins. Look, whatever happens, you won't get the blame. Fuck me, you little farm boys are safe enough. If anybody gets the blame it'll be me, and for this lot, that's a chance I'm happy to take." He dragged Si upright. "Now get the tractor down here before anybody else arrives or the fucking tide comes in. We can talk about it later."

Petal smiled at her dad and he was happy.

5

Meanwhile, other people had been out early that morning. These men left London at about four A.M., as soon as the wind dropped. They drove a large panel van with a crew cab and a hydraulic lift on the back. Careful to follow all speed restrictions and rules of the road, they traveled down the old A20 into Kent. At Ashford, they followed a series of back roads through villages like Kingsnorth and Hamstreet and then out onto Romney Marsh. At Lydd, they turned onto a narrow, unpaved road that snaked across the butt end of the marsh to the isolated stretch of shore running up to the Dungeness power station.

Dog-eared, unkempt, edged with the stunted blackthorns and the rusted wire fences of Romney Marsh, this forsaken spot of dirty, flat, rubbish-strewn strand, with its lonely birds and their lonely cries, was nobody's holiday destination. The panel van backed off the track onto the edge of the beach, and a small forklift with rubber tires was unloaded and stood beside it.

Four beefy guys walked up and down shouting expletives at one another: "What the fuck?" "Where the fuck?" "It ain't fucking here!" "It's got to be fucking here!" "It's fucking not!" "Keep fucking looking!" They walked the length of the beach right up to the chain-link fencing separating the world from the Dungeness power station. Nothing.

After the days of storm there was plenty of flotsam and jetsam but not what they were sent to collect. Back and forth they went, moaning and bitching but unwilling to accept what appeared to be the truth. Especially Simp, who'd have to tell Carter when they returned. Eventually they trudged back to the vehicle and headed off, back to their beloved South London, empty-handed and empty-headed from too much sky and too much fresh air.

Later, back in the city, Simp explained everything to Carter several times over and his head hurt. Carter always wanted everything right, but Simp knew things didn't always go that way. Carter was like a brick wall with anti-climb paint. Simp tried to tell him, but the words just slid off. Now Carter was on the phone to Colombia and he wasn't happy. "What do you mean, you can't do nothing! We paid for a delivery and we ain't got it!"

The phone was on speaker and Simp could hear the Colombian's soft, accented English: "What can we do? It's a loss for us all. It's the business we are in. It happens. I have spoken with the captain and he threw the stuff overboard as planned, but your weather... the weather was extreme."

Carter's face became suffused with blood, and while he tried to control the anger in his voice, it didn't quite work. "Why did he throw the bloody stuff off then?"

There was a moment of silence before the Colombian replied, and when he did, his voice was so gentle, so sibilant, it was dangerous. "Ah, what was he to do, eh? Carry it to port and call you? He knows nothing except where to throw it overboard. We all have money invested. All you have lost is your deposit. We have lost a whole shipment. What can any of us do? We all just have to shrug our shoulders and accept our losses. In my country that is what we call an act of God, ha ha ha."

Carter heard the menace, closed his eyes, and gritted his teeth. When the goodbyes were done, Carter threw the phone down and turned red-faced to Simp. "It just ain't no good trying to argue with those South American types, they're just fucking gauchos with an AK."

Simp wanted to say something that would help, but he'd known Carter since junior school and knew there was nothing but a random act of violence that would calm the man. As he was the only one there, he figured he may as well get it over with. He shrugged and said, "It worked all right the last time, boss."

Carter picked up the heavy-duty stapler on his desk and flung it at Simp's head. It missed, bounced off the wall, and fell to the floor. "I know that—don't you think I don't know that, you cunt!"

Carter pulled open the deep bottom drawer of the desk, took out a bottle of whiskey and a glass.

Simp said, quietly, "Boss, it's early, only just past midday. You know what your doctor said."

Putting the whiskey down on the desk, Carter picked up a large glass ashtray and, holding it like a Frisbee, flexed his arm in Simp's direction. Simp backed up against the office wall, near where the stapler had fallen. He was a big man, but he was making constant, quick little movements, adjusting himself to the stretch of Carter's arm, ready to duck. He felt in his jacket pocket for the bottle of Carter's pills.

Carter looked at his arm and the ashtray in his hand and, dropping it back down onto the desk, seemed to lose heart. With a sigh he poured himself half a glass of whiskey and swilled it down. "This ain't no time to be listening to no quack! That deposit, that's near a hundred fifty thousand pounds lost." He poured another drink. After a couple of minutes, the alcohol seeped into Carter's bloodstream and he began to think. Simp picked up the stapler and put it back on the desk. Letting out another a long sigh, Carter said, "All right, Simp, run it by me again."

Not wanting to be too close to the simmering volcano, Simp went back and stood near the door. "Well, boss, like I told you, me and the boys went down there, just like before. We had the truck and the forklift and we walked that beach, honest, backward and forward. We looked everywhere. Nothing."

Quiet for a minute, Carter sipped his drink. "All right, all right, so it wasn't there, right? But like the sea's the sea, right? Everything comes ashore somewhere, even those stupid bottles people fuck into the sea with some half-arsed note in it."

Simp said, "I know what you mean, boss, like what's the point if the bottle ends up someplace where they don't even speak English."

Carter slammed the glass down on the desk. "Shut it, you stupid cunt, I ain't talking about bloody bottles! What I'm saying is those fucking bales must have come ashore somewhere, right?"

When Carter was like this, Simp got nervous. A mood like this was all right when they had to hurt somebody. Simp knew exactly what to do then. This was different. He took a deep breath and said the first thing that came into his head. "It was that wind that fucked things up, boss."

Carter shook his head in desperation. "I know that—don't you think I don't know that. What I want to know is: Where is the fucking stuff now?!"

At a loss, Simp stood by the door looking down at the floor, one hand down his track suit bottoms, idly scratching his crotch. It was a habit, like a tic, he'd picked up in prison, and it gave him comfort in fraught situations.

Carter drank more, eyed him, and said, "Stop doing that, you're worse than a bloody dog."

Simp straightened up and put his hands behind his back.

Carter wasn't what you would call a big man, but he was dapper and mean. He'd started young, him and Simp, mugging other kids at school for their dinner money. It had been his idea and it was simple. Kids scare easy, most adults do too. He'd based their career on it. Together, Carter and Simp had graduated from housebreaking to armed robbery, mostly post offices and security vans. No-fear merchants. They went in, they went out, they shook it about, and to Carter nothing had ever seemed to matter. Even when he married nothing changed.

Then suddenly, when his daughter, Amber, was born, Carter—a man who'd always prided himself on his lack of sentiment—was stricken with love. It went against the grain and he didn't know what to do with it. Simp told him to just be careful. At first Carter had been amazed by her helplessness and then by her beauty and finally by her simple needs, and he almost thought of going straight, though even as he thought it, he knew that it could never happen. Simp suggested they moved sideways into the relatively calm waters of drug dealing: hash, marijuana, amphetamines. He didn't do street—other people did that for him. He kept several steps away, but Amber wasn't stupid; she had it figured by the time she was twelve. As Simp had pointed out to him several times down the years, he could never be what the world called a good father. But he had tried in his own way. He'd spoiled her. Now she'd walked out of her school at exam time, refused to go back, and he didn't know what to do.

Carter said, "Get me a map."

Simp went out to the car, came back with a map and handed it to Carter, who spread it out across the desk. He ran his eyes along the Kent coastline and finally jabbed a finger at the shoulder of land between Winchelsea and the power station at Dungeness, where Simp and the boys had been that morning. The shoulder of land jutted out into the Channel like a natural breakwater, with the power station at its far extremity, and from there the land swept around into the long curve of St. Mary's Bay, with Folkestone at the far end and Dymchurch in the middle.

Running his finger along the coastline, Carter mused, "So, they were supposed to turn up here, right, and if they didn't wash up there, where did they end up?"

Not wanting to go through the whole story again, Simp tried to sound contrite: "I don't know, boss, honest. Ask any of the boys, there was nothing there."

His line of thought broken, Carter glared. "That was what they call a rhetorical question, you fuckwit, it don't need an answer."

Simp wasn't stupid—far from it—but it had always suited Carter to have someone to roar at.

Looking down at the map, at the curving coastline between Folkestone and Dungeness, he said, "Well, they must have turned up someplace. So either they're still sitting on a beach somewhere or some clever cunt can't believe his luck. I'm telling you, whoever it is, their fucking luck'll change when I get hold of 'em!" He squinted down at the map and jabbed his finger into the middle of Stickle. "What's this place?" Removing his finger, Carter bent over the little splotch of land. "Look at the end of that place!" He beckoned Simp over. "Look at that! The beach at the end of that island is like a fucking scoop. Fuck me, if anything gets fucking blown off fucking course, I bet it ends up there. Get the limo, let's go to Kent and have a look."

At the door, Simp stopped. "Shall I get the boys?"

Carter shook his head. "No. Let's go down quiet like and have a gander, see what's what. We can always send the boys down later."

6

Using the forklift on the front of the tractor, Si loaded the bales onto the trailer. Dick Stick and D.C. waved their arms, but when he had to turn with the heavy trailer on the wet sand, he took Petal's instructions, and she rode in the tractor with him back to the farm. One side of her was pushed up against him in the narrow cab. They didn't talk, but Si was happy. In the barn, Si and D.C. covered the bales with a couple of big blue tarps.

By now Si was ravenous. The bacon sandwich earlier was what Si considered a starter breakfast, an ancillary snack and something just to keep him going while waiting for the real breakfast to come along. He headed into the house, where he removed his boots and hung his hat on the stand in the hallway. But even before he reached the kitchen Si knew something was wrong. There was a certain silence. The sort that hangs in the air. Ominous. The kind of silence that reminded him of childhood misdemeanors discovered and his father sitting at the kitchen table, waiting.

And he wasn't wrong. John Newman had watched the little episode from the window at the top of the stairs. He didn't know what was in the bales but guessed it was something scavenged from the beach, because D.C. had followed the tractor into the yard on his bike, and if D.C. was involved, it was possibly something dubious. If it was, he just wanted to know.

Si wasn't good at telling lies, especially to his father. John Newman got straight to the point: "What was that in the barn?"

Si scratched his head and studied his socks. He took up a frying pan and put it on the stove. At the fridge he took out sausages and black pudding. Without looking at his dad, he said, "Just some stuff D.C. found washed up on the beach." He got eggs and sparked up the stove, splashed a bit of oil into the pan.

John said, "What exactly?"

Although Si's father was an easygoing man, if he asked a direct question, he expected an answer. Si knew that and said, "Do you want some breakfast?"

A negative silence. Into the pan went three sausages. Enough for one. The sausages sizzled. Si sighed.

John Newman said, "Is it something to do with drugs?" At the stove, Si's back stiffened as John added, "I've known you smoked for a long time now."

Without turning, Si said, "It's only a bit of weed, Dad."

John laughed. "What about the magic mushrooms?"

After rolling the sausages around in the pan with the spatula, Si took a tin of beans from the shelf, applied the tin opener, reached for a small saucepan from the cupboard below, poured the beans in, and put a light to the gas. He wasn't going to talk about magic mushrooms with his dad. No way!

John Newman said, "I've taken them."

Shocked, Si finally turned to face his father. "What?! When? Who with?"

John Newman ignored his son. "Some of the conscientious objectors took them when they lived here. One of them told me that back when the Druids were around, long before the Romans ever came, part of the initiation for the priests and warriors was to be given a large dose of psilocybin mushrooms—see, I even know the right name—and be placed in a water-filled stone coffin with just a reed to breathe through and left overnight. By morning they were supposed to have composed and memorized a hundred-verse ode, which they had to recite when they got out."

Si poked his sausages, adjusted the heat under the beans, slid a few slices of bacon and black pudding in the pan, and listened like any son listens to his father: negligently, focused only on his own interests. "Yeh, yeh, that was the Druids, Dad, but who did you take them with?"

John shook his head. "That doesn't matter. It's not about that. It's about understanding that nothing is new. Look, my grandfather was raised a Quaker and my father still held a lot of their beliefs. That was why he decided to make the farm a co-op for the duration of the war."

Si had heard all the grandad and great-grandad stuff before and turned back to poke his cooking breakfast.

John Newman continued anyway. "You think you are alternative because you smoke a bit of dope! Try standing against a whole country, against the mass of public opinion, against almost everybody. Those conscientious objectors were real outsiders. My father was..." He paused. "...so strong for what he did. Imagine living in a small community like this for the duration of the war and even after—people didn't let him forget it, you know. That kind of prejudice, well, any kind of prejudice doesn't end. I didn't really realize back then, but my dad, your grandfather, was a very brave man."

A couple of eggs were cracked into the frying pan and Si let him rattle on. All the time he was talking about the past, Si didn't have to talk about the present, and anyway, he didn't really want to remember his grandfather and the way he was all wasted until he was just bones and skin before he died. Or how the funeral had meant nothing to him. Back then, in his mind, it was like the old man was still sitting in his chair in the kitchen, and anyway, he was only eight and almost nothing meant anything from way back then, same with his mother. And his dad was still talking.

"I was only about nine when the war started, but I was old enough to see what was going on. The conchies, they weren't country people. My dad had to teach them everything. Some came and worked hard, but mostly they were London people, artists or would-be artists and all that, but that's not even fair on them. Mostly they were good people with strong beliefs but not really up to country life, and the work was harder back then.

"By the time the war ended I was fifteen or so, and in a way the conchies had altered the way I looked at things. I think living with so many different people, in what I guess you'd call a commune these days, opened me up at an early age to ideas. The one thing those people could do was talk!"

Si started to giggle involuntarily.

"They could talk! Check yourself!"

There was a coffee cup on the table. John picked it up and passed it to Si. "Make some fresh, and you can laugh, and maybe it doesn't seem like it to you because I've mostly stayed on the island, but I have a philosophy. Why do you think I gave Julie and D.C. the cottage? Why do you think I let D.C. move his trailer into the high field when they split up? I mean, you know I've never charged them a penny rent. You know that, don't you?"

That was it. Si knew instinctively the mushroom thing had to be with either D.C. or Julie. Under his breath, Si said, "Julie." John shot him a glance, but Si was back turning and poking various things on the stove. Pretty soon the breakfast was cooked and he was shoveling it onto a plate: two perfect eggs over easy and black pudding, thick slices of home-cured bacon and the homemade sausages, baked beans. Things were going pretty good. He sat at the table opposite his dad and began to eat.

Sometimes living on an island wasn't all it was cracked up to be. Like your dad knowing everything you got up to. Like seeing Dick and Petal together almost every day. And, like now, the past was always there, ready to tip over into a chat about his mother, and Si didn't really want to talk about her. Sometimes it was like his dad needed to remember just to connect with the present. Si didn't get it, but it didn't seem to matter. Once John had told him, "That's right, you've heard it all before and you'll hear it again and probably again after that. It's where you come from, it's your history, and one day you'll be telling your own kids." At twenty-two, to Si, history was still a short thing.

Si had never known his mother. Well, not so it mattered. She died. He was less than two. He knew. He'd always known. He'd been told, and his dad had loved his mother, yeh, yeh, and he'd heard it all, how they met and how she died. That didn't mean he knew her. Most people didn't understand that. He was supposed to miss his mother, but how could he miss someone he never really had? How could he love someone he didn't know?

Leaving the Julie thing in the air because he didn't know what else to do with it, John Newman said, "Do you think I've never met people like D.C. before? 'Bohemians' is what they were called in my father's day. In fact, D.C. still calls himself a bohemian, would you believe it! Mostly they don't cause trouble, they don't hurt nobody—none of those hippie types do—oh, I know what they smoke. It doesn't bother me. I've known and seen worse." He rolled his eyes and then fixed a dark look on his son. "Now, tell me the truth about what you've put in our barn or I get Paloney."

Si didn't want to explain, and why would he? He wished D.C. or Petal was there to tell it, because whatever it was, they would tell it better, and knowing whatever he said wouldn't ever satisfy his dad, Si placed his knife and fork quietly on the table and, in a slow hiss, blew a long breath between his teeth. "Well, D.C.... well, not just D.C. but Petal and Dick."

John nodded. "Dick Stick?"

Si picked up his cutlery again. No sense in the rest of the food getting cold. "Yeh. Well, anyway, whoever. Between them they found these bales on the beach and wanted me to put them in the barn."

John Newman tilted his head a little to one side. A question unasked is still a question. Si stuffed food into his face. John Newman said, "I know that. I watched you. What's in the bales?"

Suddenly thirsty, Si pushed back his chair and grabbed a carton of juice from the fridge and a glass, because the one thing—well, one of the things—his dad couldn't stand was drinking from the carton. He filled the glass, finished it in three gulps, and began to try to eat again, but John placed a hand on his.

"What's in the bales?"

Si took his hand out from under, stuffed sausage and black pudding into his mouth, and, as he chewed, mumbled, "Marijuana, Dad. Dope."

John Newman shook his head and sighed. The truth and what he'd half guessed collided, and he didn't know what to say or what to do about it.

Into the silence, Si said, hopefully, "Look, don't get worried, I'm sure they've got a plan. In fact Petal already has an idea. She wants to call a meeting."

Newman wanted to shout and shake Si, but instead he eyed his son in the way one looks at a complete idiot and snapped, "Wants to call a meeting! What the hell about? Come on, Si, this isn't just a bit of weed. This is a prison sentence—for both of us."

He hadn't really thought it through, but Si liked the idea of the whole island taking control and sticking two fingers up at the council, and other factors were involved. He liked the idea of getting closer to Petal. To his dad, he said, "But you're not involved."

With a shake of his head, John Newman said, "The stuff is on our land and ignorance is no defense in law, and anyway, I know it's there, don't I?"

Everything his dad said was true. But there were still buts. One was the island had survived historically by dodgy means, and times were beginning to look hard again. Another was at least a third of the inhabitants smoked, and they were only the people he knew about. Others kept it on the low. The idea of a co-op could look good to all of them. There were other buts, but Si couldn't be bothered to think of them. Instead, he said, "But, Dad, Petal has an idea." Newman made to interrupt him but Si held up his fork and pressed on: "Wait, wait, look, she thinks we could sell it and buy the ferry and run it for ourselves—you know, like something that would benefit the whole island. I'm not really explaining it very well, but like a co-op or something."

No, for his father, Si had explained it very well. He'd watched his son with Petal ever since they were kids. He said, "It's Petal, isn't it?"

Si shook his head and lied: "That's not it." The notion that anybody could guess or know how he felt for Petal mortified Si. Jumping up, he took his plate and emptied the scraps of his breakfast into the bin by the sink.

John smiled and shook his head slowly. "Do you think I'm blind? Anyway, where's that bloody coffee?"

Si smacked his forehead. He'd forgotten the coffee. Annoyed that the way he felt about Petal was so obvious, Si grabbed the little Italian coffeemaker and, opening it up, emptied the grounds into the bin, washed it out, repacked it with fresh coffee, filled the lower half with water, screwed it back together, and put it on the stove. He wasn't annoyed at his father really but at himself. He had every right to feel the way he felt about Petal, and yet he somehow cowered from admitting it to himself or anyone else—an emotionless lunk tending the cows and sheep. Now, the bales—something of almost no interest to him three hours ago—were gathering meaning.

He quickly shifted things around in his head, the way people do, and told himself it wasn't all about Petal and how he felt; it was more, much more. All right, people in the past had world wars to fight and mad fascist politics to rail against, and maybe he didn't have anything like that, but couldn't he have a philosophy? Couldn't his ideas be on a small scale? What did they call it, microeconomics or micro-politics or micro-something, or was it macro?

D.C. told him ages ago that everything was political, even having a crap. At the time he'd laughed, and D.C. had pointed out that every time he wiped his arse, he was depleting the world's forests. Si loved the island and the farm and he didn't want to leave. Watching the coffee slowly come to a boil, Si thought about how someone like Petal would talk to his father.

When the coffee was ready, Si poured them both a cup. He rested back against the sink and tried. "You talk about your father and your grandfather and all that stuff, but what about you, what about now, when our whole way of living's threatened? It's different times now. Maybe Petal's idea could work, who knows? Whatever happens, we can't leave here, Dad, it's our home. All right, you reckon you have a philosophy. What is it, what's it called?"

John Newman rubbed a hand over his face, suddenly at odds to explain his own philosophy on life for fear of looking stupid. "It's not got a name, it's a way of being—I try to treat people as I'd like to be treated."

Si remembered Mrs. Doasyouwouldbedoneby, from *The Water-Babies*, and grinned cheekily at his dad. "Who are you, Mr. Doasyouwouldbedoneby?"

John said, laughing, "Well, really, in a way, stupid as it sounds, yes. Like I said, that was why I gave D.C. somewhere to live."

Si couldn't help a giggle. "Is that how it works with Julie too? Do as you would be done by."

John waved a dismissive hand at his son and said, easily, "What? It's got nothing to do with Julie."

Father and son smiled at each other and thought about mother and daughter, Julie and Petal. John wasn't really worried about the bales in the barn—probably no one else knew. He thought for a few moments and figured whatever was going to happen to the stuff, it would be better if he at least knew what was going on. He said, "How would it be if we had a little meeting to discuss having a meeting?"

7

Petal was excited. It was a mad idea, and when she'd come up with it she was only trying to annoy her dad, but now, now the bales were safe in the barn, she began to see things more clearly. Maybe there was a way, perhaps they could do something, maybe the idea of a co-op wasn't completely mad.

Moving to the island from London when she was nine was one of the best things that had ever happened to Petal, and now it was home and she didn't intend to leave, no matter what. Like everyone on Stickle, she'd been left numb by the news and unable to see how she or anyone could fight the cuts. She knew there weren't even enough people living on the island to mount a decent demonstration and doubted there would be anyone to listen anyway. The rest of the country didn't know Stickle existed. The government may have decided the island was no longer financially viable, but the people who lived on Stickle had chosen it, despite its shortcomings. Home was where the heart was.

The residents liked their semi-isolation, their cutoff from the mainstream, and as a group, they did not function. The blow-ins and the younger islanders came together to party or to queue to collect their dole at the post office; the older residents, for church coffee mornings and to queue at the post office to collect their pensions. It wasn't as though people weren't friendly—they were—but they liked to keep themselves to themselves. As Petal saw it, the bales of dope were the only chance they had to take control, to own and run the ferry, to keep the island alive, and although she hadn't yet figured out how to do it, she needed to find a way to bring the people together. It wasn't just about the kids getting to school or the whole financial well-being of the island.

When Dick dropped Petal off at Julie's cottage, they kissed. He said, "I better get back, there's bound to have been wind damage to the polytunnels and stuff like that." He glanced at his watch. "It's nearly nine, Dad's probably going nuts. I'll have to get things on the go."

Petal touched the side of Dick's face gently with the palm of her hand. Most people didn't realize how hard he worked. He was a good guy and she knew she took advantage of that, but he didn't seem to mind.

Because of the way he dressed, some people, including herself and his father, sometimes treated Dick like a fool, but he was far from that, and she knew the truth was the farm wouldn't function without him. The farm relied on casual labor. Henry Stick had alienated most of the casual workers over the last few years with his bad attitude, to the point where they would deal only with Dick. He organized the pickers, sorted their wages, and prepared most of the farm accounts to make sense of the black economy, before they went to the real accountants on the mainland.

Petal had enough of school by sixteen and, like most of the blow-ins on the island, collected her Social Security and worked casually on the Sticks' farm, when needed, picking fruit and veg in the summer and cutting sprouts and cauliflowers and packing potatoes in the winter. That was how she got together with Dick.

It was also true that there weren't that many fanciable people on the island, which made her wonder if a lack of choice didn't make her relationship with Dick a compromise. Petal didn't like the idea of that, but then she wasn't sure what love felt like either. She was pretty sure she wasn't in love with Dick, and she doubted if he was really in love with her, whatever he said. It was convenient for them both. Was that bad? It wasn't cynical or calculated or anything like that. They'd known each other as friends for years, liked each other and got on well. A lot of relationships were based on less. A couple of years ago, D.C. had told her, "You can have your own ideas and your own beliefs an' all, but they don't matter a fuck. It all depends on where you were born, where you live, and the prevailing culture." After Dick had driven away, Petal turned and went into her mother's cottage. The things her dad said annoyed her sometimes, especially if he was right.

The living room and the kitchen were one big space with a closed staircase running up one wall to the two bedrooms above. The bathroom was a little add-on at the back of the kitchen. They'd lived alone there ever since D.C. moved to the trailer. It was a small space and there weren't many secrets between mother and daughter.

Julie was on the couch, not exactly prone but resting easy. Stoned. Sometimes Petal felt older than both her parents. With a shake of her head, she laughed and sighed at the same time. "Dad's already been here, right?"

It was nine in the morning. Julie propped herself up on an elbow. "Yeh, he dropped a handful off on his way by. It's good."

Throwing her jacket onto the bench beneath the window, Petal picked up the teapot from the coffee table and felt the side. It was almost cold. She emptied it, switched on the kettle, and flopped down on the couch beside her mother. "Well, at least you could skin up, Mum."

Julie rolled a joint and they smoked it and drank tea. They talked about Petal's idea. She asked her mother, "What should I do?" At that moment, Julie didn't know. She'd been in a co-op once back in London but it was all a bit hazy. She agreed with Petal, but would everybody else? Julie hugged her daughter and they snuggled into each other, touching temple to temple.

Julie said, "It could all go wrong. Some of the people, you know, the ones that have been here for generations, may not see things the way we do. They don't like drugs and a good few of them don't like us blow-ins anyway, you know that. Your boyfriend's dad for one." She nodded slowly. "You know, if you go out on a limb you better be careful what limb you go out on."

Petal giggled. "That sounds like some bit of tosh Dad would come out with."

Julie gave a stunted little laugh. "Well, we did live together for quite a long time. Look, D.C. may be an awkward git, but you know he's got a good heart and he loves you."

Pulling herself a little away from her mother, Petal fixed her with a look. "A good heart? You know he wants to keep it all for himself and sell it."

With a grimace, Julie said, "Yeh, he did mention that."

They both sighed and were silent for a moment. Petal said, "What's he like?"

Julie laughed. "He's like you—but dafter. Don't worry, he'll come around in the end."

They made more tea and some toast. Julie suggested Petal go to the library in Dymchurch and see if there was a book on co-ops. She said, "From what I remember it was all deadly dull: quorums, chairpersons, and a secretary taking minutes."

Petal said, "What's a quorum?"

Julie laughed again. "I've no idea."

They chatted on. Out of the blue, Petal asked her mum, "Why couldn't I have had a normal dad? One that went to work and came home and didn't keep saying things. I mean, what was all that when I was young and he wouldn't let me call him Dad?"

There wasn't really an answer to that. Julie shrugged and kissed her daughter on the cheek. "What can I say? It was a sixties-seventies vibe, know what I mean? We thought we were doing things differently."

"Yeh, yeh, I heard it all from Dad: there was a counterculture once, but now it's just an over-the-counter culture, blah, blah."

They both laughed. After a little while, Julie said, "Anyway, everything looks weird when you look back on it."

Unable to help herself, Petal had a gentle little dig. "Like free love. What was that?"

Julie licked a couple of papers together and, shaking her head, began to build another joint. "Who knows, in thirty or forty years the sixties and seventies will look even stranger than they are beginning to look now."

8

After Dick dropped off Petal he went home to face the day ahead, when all he really wanted was to go to bed. His father wasn't in the house, probably already out stalking the farm for damage. Firing up the bike again, Dick began to tootle about the farm, in between the rows of polytunnels and greenhouses, around the finely tilled fields of strawberries and runner beans, assessing any damage and keeping an eye out for his father.

When Dick found him, Henry Stick was ripping lengths of thick plastic sheeting from the frame of a wind-damaged polytunnel. He stopped and pointed the Stanley knife he was cutting the plastic with at Dick. "Did you see? There's a couple more damaged. We need people here to help get this straight. It's going to take a couple of days at least. Get three or four of those hippie fuckers over here. There's fresh plastic in the barn for the tunnels, and we'll have to cover the broken glass in the greenhouses with the plastic sheeting as well, until I get the glass cut. Some of the beans need re-staking, and the bird mesh on the soft fruit bushes has blown away." Stopping suddenly, he stared at his son as though he'd only just noticed him. "State of you. Where have you been?"

Dick sighed, turned off the bike's motor, and went over to help. He loved his father and hated him at the same time. He'd like things to change because of the love he felt, but he couldn't break out because of that little bit of hate. He didn't understand it. He'd tried, but with his dad nothing ever got resolved. Once, when they were both drunk, his dad got all maudlin and told him, "Everybody leaves me."

Taking hold of the plastic, Dick pulled it taut while his dad slashed, and together they ripped off a whole section and, dragging it away from the tunnel, folded it roughly and dumped it beside the path. They worked together for half an hour or more until the tunnel was stripped.

Dick had understood, that time they were drunk, his dad was feeling sorry for himself and talking indirectly about his wife, Dick's mother, even though, according to his dad, he never talked about her. In reality, it was Dick who couldn't talk about his mother because his dad would throw a moody if he did.

Dick said, "I'll get some breakfast, then I'll go and check a couple of people out—but don't expect anyone to come to-day."

That didn't really satisfy Henry Stick but nothing much did. He wanted to gyp and moan. Instead, he sighed and then shouted uselessly after his son's retreating back: "Make sure you get them here tomorrow!" His rages and anger were useless and he knew it. His aging body told him so, and any-way, what was the point? He knew Dick was a good lad. It was just hard—hard for him to live with someone, to bring him up, to love him, when the way he looked reminded him of the wife he'd lost.

Moving on to the next tunnel, and again slashing away with the knife, Henry thought about his wife and his own failures. He'd been selfish and insensitive back then, and he knew, deep down, that he hadn't changed all that much. For eighteen years he'd raised Dick alone. He'd done his best but knew it wasn't always good enough. Something in him had died when Sylvia went, something lovable he'd never got back, and it hurt. He stopped what he was doing, straightened up, and looked about. The farm was a burden to him and always had been. Aimlessly, he mooched down the center of the ruined tunnel, righting the battered tomatoes against the canes. The tomatoes were mostly still green. He touched them gently and the musty smell of them filled his nostrils. He didn't hate everything.

Once, before he'd come back to the island, he'd been a different type of man: he'd had friends, he was open, he'd been the sort of man who could attract a girl like Sylvia. Sylvia was a London girl. That was where they'd got together, lived together, loved together. London was another world then, and now. He should have known, should have seen Sylvia could never be able to live on the island, but ego and natural-born arrogance was blinding. It was obvious to him now that they could probably have been happy living a different life, in London or somewhere else. He could have been a different man, but everybody is blind and stupid in his own way.

Henry Stick didn't have to come back to Stickle. He could have just left his dad to die and sold the lot, but he didn't, he did what the Sticks had always done: hunkered down on the island. But Sylvia wasn't one for hunkering. Five years and she was gone, and he'd never really gotten over it. Maybe he'd been wrong, but he wouldn't let her take Dick, wouldn't, for a while, so much as let her contact him. As though she could be forced back by emotional blackmail. That stupid idea had blown in the wind a long time back, but either way, none of it had made him happy. Sometimes he couldn't remember being really happy, happy the way he'd been with Sylvia, and sometimes life was just drudgery, going around and around, doing the same old things, and it hurt. No, he'd never really gotten over losing Sylvia.

At the far end of the tunnel there was a standpipe. He turned it on, ran it for a few seconds, and, bending down, sucked water straight from the tap. Of course, Henry could see things differently when he chose. Then he could pat himself on the back. He'd done good; he'd put his shoulder to the wheel, taken responsibility, and brought his son up, all by himself. Some man for a man. But then most people would have done that for a dog. He loved Dick—didn't always know how to show it, but he did. How his son managed, what he felt, Henry didn't know, and now, although they had never talked about it, he could tell his son wanted to leave. It was inevitable. He didn't want to be left alone and didn't need to be told that these days he couldn't manage the farm by himself. He splashed water on his face and went back to cutting away the polythene.

When D.C. had called him a king in his own kitchen, he'd been right. Little big man. The truth was Henry didn't want to be anything very much anymore. It was like he'd spent the best part of his life angry and now he didn't know why. The idea of change frightened him, yet somewhere a distant part of him hankered for something different, wanted Dick gone, wanted to get on and deal with what would be left. Henry had made plans. He'd put money aside for Dick, so if or when he did decide to leave, the lad would be free. If worse came to worst, he'd get a manager in and sit back. Whatever trouble the future held for himself, he didn't want Dick to have to return, the way he'd done.

Back in the house, Dick made himself an egg and bacon sandwich with a dab of brown sauce. He cooked the bacon crispy. He made tea and sat near the warmth of the Rayburn to eat. It was true, Dick did want to leave the island. He felt restricted. It wasn't about his father, although he didn't help. It was more about the way people treated him because they'd known him most of their lives. Like he didn't matter because they knew him so well. If they laughed while they insulted him, it was all right and he wouldn't be hurt. Either that or they didn't care when they hurt him. And that was just his friends.

Like with Petal. When he'd asked her what she'd said to Si to make him agree to take the stuff up to the barn, she'd given him a big, wide-open grin and said, "I don't have to do anything to get Si to help me." Not that he was jealous of Si, not really; they had been best mates for years. But so had Petal, and she'd ended up with him and he was lucky. Could just as easily have been Si. Had her feelings changed? Sometimes it did seem to him when people knew you too well, they forgot about your feelings.

Friends thought Dick was scared of his dad, but he wasn't exactly—maybe a bit when he was young, but for all his temper, moods, and bluster, his dad had never raised a hand to him. His father pained him, though, for all sorts of reasons. High blood pressure, for one. His drinking, for another. The fact that without help organizing the pickers, the accounts, and transport to the wholesalers, the farm would fold. Dick may have wanted to leave, but he just didn't know how to leave his old dad in the lurch.

Dick went to the bathroom and washed the gel and some of the crazy color out of his hair, until his pride and joy was just a drab mullet. Putting on the crash helmet, he set out to gather the workers, ready for the morning.

9

It was midafternoon before Carter and Simp arrived in Dymchurch. They parked the car and checked the ferry time. There was almost an hour to wait. Carter twitched and went into one: "Why? Bloody thing's just sitting there. Typical. The moment you fucking leave London nothing works right. No wonder the rest of the country's skint! Don't give me that north-south divide or that city/country shit. Get it together, you fucking carrot crunchers!"

They went to the pub and Carter had two quick doubles. Simp had a glass of ginger beer. After, they stood on the quay and looked out to sea with their hands in their pockets, waiting. They looked completely out of place.

Carter was wearing a moss-green mohair suit with thin lapels, five-button cuffs, a twelve-inch center vent, and straight-legged trousers. His shirt was a white button-down of soft cotton; the tie was thin, in muted stripes of earth red, bruised blue, and green. His shoes were dark burgundy brogues. If someone had planted a porkpie hat on his head and stuck him in a silly pose, he'd have looked like the old-time member of a new-time ska band. He was dressed the same way as when he was twenty but twenty-odd years older. He was thin, five ten, and mostly sprung tight. He could still carry it off.

Simp, on the other hand, was a big man, six four, brick shithouse style but with a soft little-boy face. Although Carter was a dangerous man, Simp had been doing Carter's dirty work since their playground days. It was just a job to him, the same way as some people are carpenters or shopkeepers and all that. Simp was casual in a scuffed tan leather coat that came down to his knees. He wore it open over a baggy Hawaiian shirt with parrots on it and was wearing trainers and Levi's.

After a little while Carter pointed to a smudge out on the horizon. "Is that it out there?" Simp looked at him and waited. Carter nudged him. "I said, what the fuck is that?"

Simp started. "Sorry, boss, I thought that was one of them rhetorical questions."

Sometimes it seemed to Simp he'd known Carter forever, and actually he almost had. It was what clever people called a symbiotic relationship. He knew that. It was need and want, help and hindrance, all held in a fine balance. A bit of love thrown in. It had started when they were barely eight years old, in the school toilets.

Carter wasn't a likable kid. Some of it wasn't his fault. His mother left him to his own devices while she drank and her men came and went. There was never much money and of what there was he didn't get his share. He was dirty and he smelled, his clothes were secondhand, he was hyperactive and prone to strike out in all directions. A bunch of the older boys soon got sick of him and had him cornered in the boys' toilets at break time. Simp happened to walk in, and Carter was punching and biting and kicking for all he was worth, but there were just too many bigger boys and he was going under.

At eight, Simp didn't think in straight lines, didn't have an overview, and he didn't know himself or what he was capable of, and he was big, even as a young one. He didn't know why he waded in—maybe because they were in the same class. To Simp, Carter was just some kid, a chavvy like himself, a boy at the back of the class. Between the two of them, they had fought the others off, and then later, they picked the boys off one by one as they came to school or as they walked home, intimidating and robbing them of the few pence they had. After that the two lads were left alone. It was the start of a beautiful friendship, and in some ways, it had been the same ever since. There were times these days, though, when Simp wanted things to change.

Mostly it was kids of various shapes and sizes on the ferry. The big, fat black BMW was the only car, and before they set off, the ferryman came over and said, "You realize this is the last ferry today, don't you?"

Carter didn't really like to be told anything or asked anything or anything. Looking the man up and down, he said, unpleasantly, "So what?"

With a shrug and a half smile, the ferryman looked Carter up and down. "Nothing." Let the London pricks find out for themselves.

Off the ferry, they tooled gently down the island's main street, past the church and the post office and the dozen or so houses. They looked at each other. Carter frowned. "I don't like this. I do not fucking like this at all, not at fucking all." The place was dead. Nothing was happening and that bothered him. Nothing happening had always bothered Carter.

On the other hand, Simp didn't see the problem. He liked the country; it had good memories. Anyway, there wasn't any point in getting paranoid. It was the country. It was quiet. That was what the country was like. He said, "Looks nice, quiet."

Carter blew air through his nose. "It's too quiet. Something's got to be going on. It's like one of those films, you know, where the whole village has a brood of these kids with weird eyes and they end up running the fucking planet."

Simp looked at him sideways and said, "Weird eyes?"

Carter didn't bother to explain and, in an attempt to look at his ease, opened the window. He took in a great snoot full of pure air and coughed. Even he had to admit it was all very picturesque and lovely, with the afternoon sun making the air all warm and creamy. But where were the people?

They drove slowly around the island's rutted roads, the high green hedgerows bursting with blooming honeysuckle, fuchsia, and sukebind. The last's heavy, sensuous scent filled the car and sent Carter into an uncontrollable fit of sneezing. "Fucking countryside."

Simp flipped him a pack of anti–hay fever tablets. "Here, here's those tablets you got last year."

Carter took out the flask he always carried and, with a swig, swallowed a couple. "Fucking countryside!"

The island was small. Having almost completed a circuit, Simp pulled into the gateway of a field. When Carter stepped out of the car, it was into something nasty a cow had left, and he complained and moaned and spent ten minutes cleaning his shoe with clumps of dock leaves and grass. In the meantime Simp spread a map out on the roof of the car. Together they looked at it this way and that, they turned it around, they cocked their heads. They weren't Boy Scouts.

Simp identified the track leading past the Newman place, down to Fishtail Bay. It was back through the village and left and left and, if it wasn't ridiculous, left and left again. As though it were his doing, Carter poked a finger on the spot Simp had indicated. "That's it. Come on, let's go and have a look."

Just because Simp and Carter didn't see anyone didn't mean they weren't seen, and whoever didn't see them the first time around probably saw them the second. First off was Paloney. With nothing better to do, he was standing looking out the front window of the police house as they passed. Simp was driving so sedately it was easy for Paloney to take down their registration. Nobody on Stickle owned a BMW. Most, including himself, relied on pedal power. Paloney didn't like what he was thinking.

Second was Postmistress P. Inside the deserted shop, she stood in the gloom looking out onto the village street. Beside her, Julian Crabbe, vicar of this parish. One of Postmistress P's hands was fondling the vicar's buttocks. Julian Crabbe was smiling. Mischievously, she said, "Ooh, look! People from another dimension."

Then there was D.C. D.C. had a spot in the Newmans' top field, about three-quarters of an acre. He tended it well and grew most of what he needed. He had chickens, enough for eggs most of the year and a few young ones for the pot. And a pig. Home was two trailers cobbled together in a T shape. D.C. was feeding the pig when he saw the BMW pass. A car like that on the island simply wasn't normal. Add that to what was in the barn—it was two and two, and D.C. didn't need telling.

Si saw them the second time around, as they followed the rutted dirt track by the Newmans' farm toward Fishtail Bay. Strangers. He thought of the police and he thought of his dad. He thought about Petal and wondered if he could talk to her. He didn't want things to go wonky.

Down on the beach, Carter and Simp walked up and down, but the tide was in and most of anything that had been there was gone now, all washed away. There were still a few tracks from the tractor and trailer. Carter pointed. "Look, it don't take some kind of fucking mastermind to figure this shit out. Someone's been down here and they've got it."

Sitting down and taking his shoes off, Simp didn't answer. Instead he smiled up at Carter, wriggled his toes in the sand, and stood up. He pointed at the sea and began to toddle off toward it. Before his feet got wet, he stopped and rolled up his jeans.

Carter mooched about. He could hear Simp squeal like a girl as the sea creamed between his toes. Carter persevered. He found some scraps of plastic and a bit of burlap and tracks in the sand. Against the odds he felt optimistic. He looked toward the sea. Simp was waving at him, trying to encourage him to have a little paddle. Although secretly Carter thought Simp was daft as a brush, he was the nearest thing Carter had to a friend and always had been, and sometimes you just had to indulge people. Or maybe it was the sea air or whatever, but on a whim, he waved back at Simp, and anyway, at that precise moment, everything looked likely. Maybe it wasn't money lost after all, and in the end he'd have a laugh on those fucking gauchos. Fudavid granck them! To Carter it was all obvious. Where else would it be? If it had washed around the headland at Dungeness, this was the first bit of land it would come to. All he had to do now was to find out who had it. The island was tiny. How hard could it be?

Like a daft Russian doing that daft Russian dance, he managed to pull his shoes and socks off without actually sitting on the sand. Sit in the sand in a mohair suit? Do be brief. He pulled his trousers up above his calves and ran toward the little white tops as they tootled in toward the beach.

The sky was all tiny, pure, almost see-through clouds, spaced out in an infinite powder blue. It was all quiet and clean and clear, and Simp could have stayed forever with his feet in the cool wet sand and the little waves rushing around his ankles. He thought about when he was a kid, the year his mum began to get really ill, and a friend of hers, Pearl, came and collected him. Pearl lived on a farm down in Padockwood in Kent. Simp had stayed down there for the whole summer. It was magic. A different world. No one called him Simp, they called him by his name, Simon, and they let him ride on the tractor and everything. It was like being free. Since then, he'd always had a soft spot for Kent. It was pointless trying to explain to Carter that he kind of liked the island: the quiet, the air that made you want to breathe. And the fact was that when you worked for Carter, having nothing happening was a relief.

Strangely enough Carter too chilled with the waves. He took a nip from his flask. The whiskey warmth in his mouth and the cool all around his feet were lovely. Out on the horizon the blue of the sky and the green of the sea made a kind of haze, and some kind of ship passed slowly across it, like a cutout cartoon from the fifties. For the smallest moment, he forgot everything. But not for long.

Chop a little block out of time—two minutes or so, not longer—and stick it in among all that quiet and sun and sea, and that was about long enough for Carter. Pulling a handkerchief from his pocket, he cleared his sinuses in a series of toots and squeaks and, taking a deep, clean breath, held it like a dope smoker and squeaked, "It's here somewhere, I can smell it! All we've got to do now is find a hotel or something and tomorrow we can—" Then, all of a sudden, air came out of him in a blast and he coughed and hacked and backed back onto the dry sand. "Fuck it, that air's too much!"

10

They drove around the island again, this time looking for a place to stay: a hotel, a bed and breakfast, somewhere, anywhere. A pub. Carter couldn't believe there wasn't a pub. There was one every hundred yards in Peckham. "What do they do when they just got to get the fuck away, out of the house or whatever?"

They stopped in the village and entered the post office. After the bright afternoon, the interior of the shop was quite dim, its outer limits indistinct. The two men set their shoulders as though some hidden threat may have been lurking in the shadows, but there was only Julian Crabbe's nervous grin as he sidled sideways away from the post office counter, while Postmistress P, with a different kind of smile, slid in behind it.

For some reason, most people on the island thought of Postmistress P as old, but she wasn't, not really, unless thirty-five is old. She dressed down, in shapeless jumpers and ankle-length skirts. Her auburn hair was braided into two plaits and pinned up on her head like some Flemish bint from another century. A large pair of horn-rimmed glasses sat as a barrier across her eyes. Her smile for Carter and Simp expressed tolerance, nothing more. She didn't like the look of them.

Penelope was her given and it was one thing, among many, she'd never quite forgiven her mother for. For her whole young life, the name had plagued her. Through most of her youth her school friends had pronounced her name *Pe-ne-lope* (as in *antelope*), but it wasn't even that. Her feelings about the name were not something rational or anything she could explain, but she never ever felt like a Penelope. They say "What's in a name?" but sometimes it's everything from the get-go.

Penelope got away. Disappeared. Built her own life from scratch. Moved, went and lived in a city with fifty thousand other runaway Penelopes, Deidres, Janes, and Ethels. There her name meant nothing. She could call herself what she liked and thought she could become anything she liked, and she could and life was good. She got a job, shared a flat. She made friends. People took her as they found her. Penelope discovered things about herself, things Stickle Island was too small for her to find, and Penelope enjoyed herself and learned what she liked and what she didn't, and life was big and open and she did pretty much whatever she liked, until the day came when her mother had a stroke.

That was the day Penelope realized the bad thoughts she had about her mother didn't amount to anything. Yes, her mother was a cantankerous, suspicious, and mean-spirited old bird, but what could Penelope do? She came home. Now, eight years on, the old girl was practically bedbound and Penelope had transformed into Postmistress P, and she stayed in the shop late most nights because she didn't want to talk to her mother or to empty the commode or to help her bathe or cook supper or do any of the things she had to do. Nonetheless she did them, day in and day out. Talking to her mother was the hard bit.

Eight years is a long time, and what with the advent of the blow-ins, most islanders didn't know or had forgotten the modern girl with short bleached hair, big earrings, and patterned tights who'd come home. After she and Julian had got to know each other, she'd shown him a picture of her London self and he'd been a little taken aback. It was the swing over the bed more than the fact that she was on it. Her hair had been red then. Her breasts all white with dark pink nipples. The short skirt she was wearing was caught in time, lifting in the forward movement. Who had a swing above the bed? That was what had got him.

He'd said, "You, um, dress very differently these days."

She'd shrugged. "I had to take over the business. No one takes you seriously in a miniskirt."

It had taken Julian Crabbe several months to realize Postmistress P had feelings for him and several weeks more to understand those feelings were carnal.

Carter tried to come on nice, like butter wouldn't melt, and Simp smiled out of his little-boy face, but Postmistress P knew there wasn't a family on the island who'd happily put this pair of dodgy fucks up for the night, except... As though on cue, Julian Crabbe, over by the tinned goods, hopped forward, all teeth and trousers and always ready to improve on his shaky relationship with God and the public. "I don't like to speak out of turn, gentlemen, but I have a spare room at the vicarage."

The two turned on him like dogs who had finally found a home. They wagged their tails and made the appropriate noises, even when the vicar explained that they would have to share a bed. A bed was better than the car, any dog knows that. As if to mollify the two men for being forced into such intimacy, Julian spread his hands out, elbows clenched to his ribs, like a man willing to take on all the world's problems— the sick, the poor, and the weak—and wrap them into his ever-loving arms. "It's humble, but I can offer you supper as well."

Carter and Simp thanked him profusely. Tosser.

11

The vicar placed the huge bowl of pasta slathered in a thick tomato sauce in the middle of the table. "Help yourselves, chaps." He cast a beneficent smile on the two men. "It is so pleasant to have unexpected guests."

Carter and Simp made the right noises, smiled, tried. Carter had the feeling that he was back in the 1950s, in one of those old black-and-white films, and pretty soon Alastair Sim would come through the door with those dodgy eyes of his.

After the food was finished, Simp helped Julian Crabbe with the washing up, and Carter, sitting in the living room, could hear the mumble of their conversation interspersed, every once in a while, with Simp's guffaw and the vicar's giggle. He didn't get it, the way Simp could talk to people, just like that. Went around smiling at people all the time, even people he was going to batter. There was no malice in him at all, and anyway, what the fuck *were* they laughing at?

Simp came in carrying a tray with three small, short-stemmed glasses on it. Carter, to whom paranoia was as natural as breathing to most folks, snapped, "What's so funny, eh?"

Simp had seen it all and moved out of the way only when objects were going to be thrown. With a shrug, he said, "Julian was telling knock-knock jokes."

He began to tell a joke but Carter cut him short. "Don't get too friendly. We ain't here to make friends."

Simp shook his head slowly. "He's given us food. He's putting us up for the night. I can't blank him—for a vicar, he's all right."

With a sniff, Carter said, "Yeh, too fucking good to be true, if you ask me! Look, someone on this island has got our stuff and it could be him out there, he's fucking weird enough." As he spoke he nodded toward the kitchen door, just as Julian came through carrying several boxes of board games and a bottle of something he called amontillado. Carter smiled as the vicar poured the sticky golden liquid into the three little glasses.

Julian Crabbe came from a soft background. He had soft parents who cared, and it wasn't until he went to his first parish of Toxteth, in Liverpool, he realized life was harsh in the soft country he thought he lived in. Julian Crabbe was a good man, a natural innocent, a man who, despite the odds, miraculously managed to believe in God. A decent man with a flaw. Julian liked to gamble.

When he was winning he saw God in the cards falling on a table, in the feel of warm dice in the palm of his hand, in the final jumps of the ball as the roulette wheel slowed, in the phony clicking stops and dancing lights of the slot machine when it loved him.

When confronted with the strange new world of Liverpool, he couldn't really deal with it. The thick dirty smell of the houses, the pinched poverty heads of the children , the worn-out women and the hard physicality of the men. Julian tried but spent his waking hours on the edge of panic. Unable to cope, he turned, as most people do, to his source of distraction. His kick. Naive, gullible, Julian gambled and got himself into an amount of debt, and people who loaned money in Toxteth expected debts to be paid. So he'd been sent to Stickle for his sin, and now, with a tiny congregation consisting mostly of a few old dears and Postmistress P, who believed in nothing, he was actually quite happy. Out of trouble and out of the way.

The two Londoners drank the amontillado down the way you drink down cough syrup and smiled through the horrendous taste, like cheap morphine addicts anticipating a Collis Browne high. For Carter's palate, the sweet flavors were all wrong, and usually Simp didn't drink at all; shandy was his limit. Julian, on the other hand, sipped the sherry. He loved it. He didn't understand why, but it was a drink that evoked feelings in him he couldn't quite chart, like Christmas, like warm nights in front of a coal fire, like TV adverts that glow with middle-class comfort, like planted false memories of things that never really existed, but he still liked it.

When it came to seconds, Carter and Simp held up their hands in protest. No please! Julian wasn't having any of it. Julian loved company. Company made an evening, brightened things up, and here on Stickle, random company was rare. It got lonely on Stickle, even with Postmistress P. Leaning forward, bottle in hand, Julian eyed them like a little daredevil and refilled their glasses, regardless.

The games came next. Carter started to gyp, and Simp, remembering the past, told Carter what he'd been told when he was a kid on the farm: "It's the country, what else you going to do?" Okay. But for a start, Carter refused outright to play Monopoly. He wasn't going to jail, even in a game. Buckaroo! was out because Simp's fingers were too big. Then they tried The Archers game, but it was just way too boring. Taking sheep to market in Borchester didn't light anyone's fire. They ended up, at Julian's suggestion, playing three-card brag.

Julian couldn't help the way he was made. He still liked to gamble and he still liked to believe God liked him to win. In Toxteth, God just wasn't on his side, but Toxteth had taught him something at least: stop if you are winning and stop if you are losing. So at about ten thirty, he stretched and yawned. He didn't like to hurry his guests but, as he point-ed out, it was the pensioners' coffee morning tomorrow and they could be quite a lively bunch. Pocketing his near fifty quid in winnings, he was happy and already thinking of Postmistress P. Carter, who had lost the bulk of the money, was quietly spitting feathers.

The bed was a big bed, and for that small mercy they were grateful. Coy as only two guys can be, Carter and Simp turned modestly away from each other as they undressed. Both had been in various government institutions in their youth and were careful not to touch each other as they set-tled in the bed.

The two glasses of sherry had Simp soon asleep, but Car-ter sat up, back against the headboard, taking small sips from his flask. The whole evening had been a failure as far as he was concerned. Uselessly he'd spent most of the time trying to pump the vicar for information about people on the is-land—the blow-ins, the locals—and how he expected those hippie types were up to all sorts, drugs and whatnot. All he discovered was that the ferry was due to be cut the following April and that his congregation was very small and made up mostly of OAPs. A big fat nothing. Not only that but Julian Crabbe had gulled him for near fifty quid. He didn't trust the vicar. The vicar was too nice and too good at cards. A well dodgy combination.

Now, as he sat in a strange bed, with a strange bed com-panion, the natural silence unnerved him and he wished he was back in London. One thing London's noise had taught Carter was that most sounds don't have a meaning, but here, in the quiet, it seemed every sound had a meaning, a purpose to be deciphered. His ears strained. His eyes searched the darkness of the room for the whisper of air creeping beneath the door, the unfathomable creaks of an old house settling for the night.

Julian Crabbe came out of the vicarage as silently as a ghost and, with the barest click, pulled the door closed behind him. Sensitized as he was, Carter heard, slipped from the bed, and pulled the curtain aside, just in time to see the vicar slither through the front gate. Carter spoke softly to himself: "Either something is going on or I'm getting paranoid to the point of paranoia."

Back in bed, he nudged Simp violently in the ribs, and, bleary-eyed, Simp spluttered, "What—what, boss?"

Carter wanted to slap him, but they were in bed together and near naked, and he didn't want to start something he couldn't finish without it getting biblical, but then again, he wasn't going to have any fucker sleeping on the job. He gave Simp another couple of digs. "Wake up!" Simp rubbed his eyes, nonplussed, and Carter snapped, "That vicar. Where's a bloody vicar going this time of night, eh?"

Simp didn't know what on earth Carter was ranting about and couldn't really listen because he was still in a torpor, so he rolled over and took most of the coverings with him. Carter tried again to rouse him; he poked and prodded, but Simp slept on.

Carter cursed. "Okay! Forget it! But I'm telling you, this island ain't right. It just ain't right."

He pulled at the blankets until he'd recaptured enough to cover himself and scrunched down in the bed. As he lay there he asked himself what a man of God was doing, going out into the night when there was nothing to go out into the night for. The more he thought about it, the more relaxed he became. Seeing Julian Crabbe scuttling away was like confirmation that his bales were out there somewhere, and that, to Carter, was almost like getting his money back, and the thought of money comforted him, always had. And so, before long, he too was snoring gently.

12

Head down but eyes everywhere, Julian Crabbe came up the garden path and, when he reached the gate, gave a nifty look right and left along the village street. It was empty. It was always empty. Beyond the sanctuary of the garden, he made a nervous stuttering run to cover the bare fifty yards to the post office and skittered down the side of the building. It was a journey Julian made several times a week, but still, he couldn't help looking over his shoulder, just in case. All clear, and so, with great care, he gently opened the unlocked back door.

In his natural innocence, Julian imagined their trysts were completely secret from the rest of the island's inhabitants, and that was perfectly true, for less than a quarter of them. The deaf, the blind, and the plain stupid saw nothing—never had, never would—and it wasn't their fault, blah, blah, but anyway, both these people were consenting adults. Man and woman fuck. Big deal! It's hardly tabloid headlines, and anyway, it was hard to keep a man of God on Stickle. Even the deaf, the blind, and the plain stupid understood that much, and understanding leads to acceptance. A-fucking-men!

The back door opened into a little lobby with a coat rack against the wall and the stairs to the right. Another door, heavily locked and bolted, went through to the shop. Julian carefully removed his shoes and began, silently, to ascend the stairs, ears straining. When he could hear Penelope's mother's rhythmic snore from the opposite end of the corridor, Julian opened Postmistress P's bedroom door.

Postmistress P was propped up in bed. The reading lamp was on and she had a copy of Henry Miller's *Nexus* in her hand. When she saw Julian's head in the crack of the door, like a tortoise poking its head uncertainly from its shell, she laid the book aside, removed her glasses, and waved him into the room.

A Liberty paisley silk scarf lay on the bedside table, and she hung it over the lamp so the light became soft and defused. The Penelope of the night was not the postmistress of the day. As Julian Crabbe came into the room, she threw back the quilt to reveal herself.

She took his breath away, always. Resplendent, this night, in a gooseberry-green split-crotch teddy coupled with fishnet stockings and a velvet bow tie. Her auburn hair was free of its plaits and flowed crinkly and light over her shoulders and breasts. The vicar wondered, briefly, as he ripped off his clothes, how he'd got so lucky.

Naked, he crawled toward her from the foot of the bed as Penelope lifted her legs and rested them on his shoulders. Julian kissed her slim ankles, her calves, her lovely soft thighs, and gently began to work his tongue into the split in the teddy...

Later, as they lay in a postcoital huddle, they discussed the two visitors. Julian Crabbe, still starry-eyed from the fifty-quid win, had noticed almost nothing about the men, only that they weren't very good at cards. He said, "They seem pleasant enough, but I can't imagine why they are here. It's a bit like they took a wrong turn and found themselves stranded. Ha, bit of a shock, I think."

Rubbing a hand gently over her lover's stomach, Penelope said, "The big one seems quite nice but the other one, Carter, I think he may have mental health problems. His eyes stick out and he can't stand still." She paused, not able to quite articulate the mixed feelings she had about Carter and Simp. With a sigh and a tug at Julian's pubic hair, she said, "They look a bit like criminals from the TV. Loan sharks or thugs or something like that. I met people like that when I lived in London. Usually they're not very nice."

Julian had come to the conclusion that Penelope's past was on a need-to-know basis. Mostly he didn't need to know, only to enjoy. God was good. He said, "One doesn't like to judge."

That gave Penelope a laugh. She jerked hard at his pubes. "You Christians! It's way too easy to say you don't want to judge, but you Christians are the worst! Well, along with every other organized religion. That's all you do, judge. You judge the individual and the masses. You judge, but I judge too, everybody judges. We do it automatically, instinctively. We judge everyone, against ourselves and the situation. It's natural." Then she started kissing him again and suddenly a lot of what she'd said seemed to make sense.

13

When D.C. was fifty feet away, Paloney stepped from the lea of a hedge onto the road. It wasn't like he hadn't done the whole thing before. He turned on the flashlight and swung the beam from side to side. Hardly surprised, D.C. pulled up beside the policeman and said, amiably, "All right, Phil?" Paloney offered his hand. D.C. ignored it, looked him straight in the eye, and said, ironically, "Fuck me, you almost frightened me to death."

PC Phil Paloney knew all of D.C.'s runnings: when he went up to the Smoke to bring back the dope he sold and most of his other comings and goings too. It was his job and he liked to keep his eyes open, and on an island as small as Stickle it wasn't hard. Being on Stickle was more like a type of community policing. All the time he'd been on the island, he hadn't made a single arrest. What he'd tried to do was make friends instead of enemies. So far it had seemed to work and he liked it. He said, casually, "Well, I thought you'd be coming this way."

D.C. spat a gob of yellow phlegm between Paloney's splayed feet and laughed. "Fuck off. Seeing as I only live in the next fucking field and there ain't exactly a lot of roads on the island, I fucking well would come this way, wouldn't I? Why don't you just wait for me up by the trailer?" D.C. shook his head. "All this palaver every time you want to visit. Leave me out! Hiding in the fucking bushes, like, who gives a fuck?"

Paloney pulled his bike from the hedge. "Well, some people do, and you wouldn't want me to get the sack, would you? You don't know who you'd get next."

With a giggle, D.C. shrugged. "Whatever!"

At the five-bar gate into the field, D.C. dismounted and, unhooking it, waved the policeman through. They pushed their cycles over to the trailer, and as D.C. opened the door, Paloney reached inside his tunic and pulled out half a bottle of vodka. "I brought this along."

With a flourish, D.C. said, "Enter, friend!"

When they were settled at the table, D.C. opened the door to the woodburning stove, tossed a couple of faggots on top of the dying embers, and slammed the cover shut. It wasn't a cold night and they didn't need the heat, but the red glow through the tiny glass windows was kind of comforting.

They sat opposite each other at the little fold-down Formica table, a shot glass of vodka each. Paloney took a lungful of smoke and passed the joint back to D.C. They were both smiling. D.C. said, "I know living on this fucking island restricts your social life somewhat, but I never imagined I'd end up liking a copper! How fucking weird is that?"

Paloney thought about the two wasted years in London with the metropolitan police. Colleagues had told him he was too honest. Mostly it had seemed to him he couldn't do right and didn't want to do wrong, and eventually he'd been transferred out of the way, to Stickle. He said, "What? I know I may be a bit of a failure as a policeman, but at least I haven't lost my humanity, and anyway, a man doesn't become another species because he puts on a uniform. That is what people call choice. It's down to the individual, not the clothes he wears."

Holding up his glass, D.C. said, "Philosophical fucker, ain't you?"

They clinked glasses and sat in silence.

The young policeman knew D.C. went up to London every month or so to bring back enough cannabis to supply the islands' heads. No one thought of it as dealing, not even Paloney. It was more a social service than an outright moneymaking venture.

After a time, Paloney said, "Anyway, what do you think?"

It had been a long day. Quite a few things had happened, and while D.C. could have taken a punt, he figured he may as well make Paloney work just a little bit. Innocently, D.C. queried, "About what?"

Paloney eyeballed him, head cocked. "You know."

"Do I?"

Paloney closed one eye and peered at D.C. "Sure you do, but what are we going to do about it?"

Speaking through a cloud of escaping smoke, D.C. said, "What? Come on, spit it out. It's like twenty questions without the fucking questions! Even you must see the bizarrity of that! How am I meant to be able to guess what you want?"

Paloney flapped a hand. "Come on, *bizarrity* ain't even a word."

D.C. countered with a pointy finger. "So what? English is a live language—words get added to the *Oxford Dictionary* every few years. Where do they come from? Someone made them up, that's where they come from, and they end up in common usage and that's how they get in the dictionary. What do you want, that we should be like the French and try to weed out every new or foreign word?" He moved his hands through the air like he was opening books and ripping out pages. "Not to be too harsh, but French is practically a dead language. Look, who really speaks French but the French? English takes in everything. We adapt and bastardize, and English is spoken everywhere in the world because of it. That's obvious, but anyway, that's not the point." He stopped talking for a moment, and even though he knew what Paloney

81

was on about, he held his hands out just like little Oliver asking for more. "Just tell me straight, what the fuck are you on about?"

Paloney laughed. D.C. often made him laugh, when he wasn't annoying him. "I may be a plonker, D.C., but I ain't stupid. Nice grass by the way, very fresh."

Paloney was still smiling, but both men knew things were in the open now. With a cough, D.C. got up from the table and, taking the joint with him, paced the length of the trailer, back and forth, before coming back to Paloney. "How did you know?"

The policeman told him, "Saw you on the beach after the storm. I wasn't sure, but later, when I saw those two down from London, well!"

D.C. nodded. "Oh, those two, yeh, I saw them all right. I hear they're staying with the vicar."

Serious now, Paloney said, "Look, there are things I can ignore, okay, but we can't have people like that on the island. This island can't become a staging post for drugs. Just tell me the truth, do you know them?"

"Fuck me, what do you take me for?!" Like a man whose reputation was pristine, D.C. eyed Paloney with disgust and flicked the joint straight at him. "You cunt. Of course I don't know who they are, but it don't take a genius to see what they are."

The joint hit Paloney on the chest and fell on the table. The policeman dusted himself down and picked it up. "Watch the uniform."

They poured out two more shots and rolled another joint. They left things on a shelf to be dealt with later and talked about the books they were reading. Paloney was reading *The Demon* by Hubert Selby Jr. and D.C. was reading Thackeray's *Vanity Fair* for the third time. D.C. talked about a bloke he'd met one time who couldn't understand why anyone would read a book more than once. But as he pointed out, what can you say to someone who doesn't understand everything is different all the time and that is what makes a book so brilliant? Words slide into your brain and mind, and the words' effect changes, depending on your emotions. A passage, a sentence, a word even, can be meaningless one month, but read a month later can devastate. D.C. said, "See, I don't believe we make many rational decisions. I reckon most decisions are emotional; we just dress them up in a rational coat and hat. But anyway, in the end, who gives a fuck? Because it's all transient. But you better talk to Petal about that thing. I think it's already out of my hands."

Paloney said, "I'm trying to talk to you."

D.C. shrugged. "Petal's got ideas. Look, what came ashore could be worth like two million or something, and Petal wants to do something, like change things, you know, for the island, for the community. Fuck me, if it was up to me I'd piss off, sell the lot, and never be seen again."

With a shake of his head, Paloney laughed and held up his glass. "You're so full of shit."

D.C. grinned and they clinked glasses, knocked back their vodka, poured more. D.C. said, "So, better speak to Petal."

After a bit more chat, they agreed to speak to Petal together.

Later, riding home in the quiet, Paloney could hear the rhythmic click of the pedals and the swooshing crunch of tires against the asphalt. Somewhere off to his left, beyond the hedgerow, the mesmeric hoot from a hunting owl came and went. On the verge, under an overhanging tree, a trio of baby rabbits sat on their haunches undisturbed and watched him pass like spectators at a race.

There was a sweetness in the air and Paloney drank it down. Blossomy smells—sukebind, fuchsia, and such—and all mixed up with a trace of ripening soft fruit. The air filled his lungs, rushed into his bloodstream, and bubbled in his brain, like the best drugs do. He thought of Albert Hofmann on his bike, and he looked up.

Night on Stickle, especially in the summer, was pure and peaceful, as good as a world new minted, and overhead, rippling chunks of buttery moon seemed to float independently from one another, segmented by bands of thin, deep purple clouds. Out in the universe, way beyond the moon, planets burned and froze, exploded, imploded, and stars fluttered and winked.

As he entered the village, a young fox, tail resplendent, ambled nonchalantly across the road in front of him and disappeared through a gap in the hedge beside the post office. There was a faint light in a bedroom window. The world was gorgeous, unpredictable, and sublime, and he thought about Postmistress P and the vicar and thought, *Good luck to them.*

14

When Julian Crabbe knocked on their bedroom door it was nearly 8:30 A.M. Both men were on their backs snoring gently. It was sweet really. Beneath the covers, Carter and Simp were holding hands. At the knock, both sat up with a start, released their grip, and looked dubiously at the other, a little worm of doubt. Carter was out of the bed in an instant, as if someone had passed an electric current through the mattress.

It wasn't that waking up holding Simp's hand had angered him, but it wasn't that it hadn't either. The fact was that he awoke most mornings ready to shove the rest of the human race aside and take whatever he wanted. It wasn't that he hated people or the rest of the world; it wasn't even anything he had a proper name for. Call it energy, desire, whatever, it was the thing that got him up in the mornings. Not this actual morning! Leave it out! Every morning. It had nothing to do with holding hands.

Simp still lay back, comfortable in the bed. The sour taste of the amontillado was still in his mouth and he wished he had a toothbrush. Carter, fully dressed now apart from his suit jacket, was flexing his shoulders in a mirror on the wardrobe door. Carter looked angry, but Simp reasoned his boss mostly looked angry. It didn't bother him. He looked at the hand that had held Carter's close up, turned it back to front, looked at the scarred knuckles and the red-blue veins beneath the skin. How on earth had it happened? He said, "What's the plan?"

As he slipped into his jacket and turned away from the mirror, Carter said, "Most people ain't got the courage of their convictions—that's what most people are like, but that ain't me, do you get me? Something's wrong here, I can feel it. We are going to find my fucking grass and teach whoever the fuck has it, and anyone else in this piss-poor place—animal, vegetable, or any other dodgy, dog-collared fucker—not to fucking fuck with me." Simp pulled himself out of bed, stretched, and as he did so, Carter pushed past him and blew air through his teeth. "Don't fucking hold my hand again, right!"

By the time Simp came down the stairs, Carter was already sat at the table and he could hear the vicar rattling the pans out in the kitchen. There was a smug, self-satisfied smile on Carter's chops. He gestured with his head toward the kitchen. "I figured out where the rev went last night."

Indifferent to Julian Crabbe's private life, Simp raised an eyebrow. Until that moment, he'd forgotten about Carter waking him in the night. He pulled a little face, nothing drastic.

Carter continued: "He's knocking off that postmistress, I'd lay money on it!"

That made Simp laugh out loud. The vicar seemed like an okay guy, but come on! He was a long drink of water and she looked kind of scary. He wondered how they made that work and he thought, for just a moment, of reminding his boss that he'd lost the best part of fifty quid to that long drink of water. Instead he said, "What makes you think that?"

Like there was something nasty running under his nose, Carter raised his top lip and sniffed. He tapped a finger against his temple. "Because I thought about it. I used my brain. That's why I'm in charge." He paused and nodded a couple of times as though, after the hand holding, the balance of power between them had been restored. He went on. "When we went in that post office yesterday, those two flew apart like..." He searched his brain for things that flew apart. Nothing. "Anyway, where else would he be going at that time of night? It's obvious, if you bother to think about it." Carter thought some more and said, "Like magnets. They flew apart like opposing magnets or atoms." Simp smiled like he was interested.

At that moment, Julian Crabbe backed into the room and Carter put his finger to his lips. There were fried egg sandwiches and a pot of tea on a tray. As he sat down, Julian dispensed big smiles at them both and rubbed his hands together. "Sorry to have to wake you so early, chaps, but as I explained last night, it's the pensioners' coffee morning and I have to get to the church." He looked at the watch on his wrist and gave a little shake of his head. "Time tramps on." He pointed to the egg sandwiches. "Poor fare, I'm afraid, but this is a poor parish."

After breakfast Simp was gobsmacked and apprehensive, as Carter followed Julian into the kitchen, insisting, "Helping with the washing up is the least I can do." The kitchen was basic and reminded Carter of the scullery in the terraced two-up two-down he'd grown up in. There was an old stone sink with a wooden draining board, open shelving on the walls, and worn cracked lino on the floor. There wasn't a washing machine, and the ancient, New World electric cooker looked like it came from the 1930s. Carter had almost forgotten what it was like to be poor, and he didn't like to be reminded.

They stood side by side, Julian up to his elbows in suds and Carter like a docile crocodile, taking the cleaned plates and utensils to dry and stack. Julian chattered on, but Carter wasn't listening. After a few minutes, he threw down the tea cloth, reached out, grabbed the vicar by the throat, and pushed him up against the wall. Carter was at least four inches shorter than Julian, but violence doesn't have a size.

The vicar flapped his arms, and little globules of soapy foam floated about the room.

Julian scared easily and immediately thought it was about the fifty quid he'd won. He stuttered and choked and wanted to tell Carter that he could have the money back, but he couldn't get the words out because Carter kept tightening his grip. His breakfast turned a slow somersault in his stomach. He'd been beaten up before and, not born to violence, he didn't like it. He felt sick.

Calmly, Carter said, "You could be wondering what someone like me is doing here. Well, like a lot of people, the storm's disrupted my business, and I lost something and now I want it back."

It seemed to Julian that perhaps his feet weren't touching the floor anymore. He had absolutely no idea what Carter was talking about. He felt like a child, inept, inadequate, and in the grip of a monster. He moved his arms and legs, but it didn't seem like he owned them anymore. A curdled, eggy sickness was beginning to creep up his esophagus. He tried to plead but Carter wouldn't let him.

Carter said, "Don't bother. Look, I saw where you went last night. You went to see the woman that runs the post office. Now that kind of thing may be all right with me, but I don't know how it sits with your bishops and their conclaves or whatever, and anyway, I don't want to be a snitch." Carter's smile became a sneer. "I'm not the complaining type."

All of Julian's stomach was up in his throat now. Fear had his guts, and only Carter's grip stopped a mess pouring from his mouth. Julian was a coward and he knew it. He would never be able to withstand torture. It wasn't a failing—most people are just built that way and don't like pain.

Carter said, "So, tell me now, who on this island is a bit dodgy, you know, likes to smoke a bit of that wacky 'backy? Who do you know who's a bit like that? Come on, help yourself and help me here. I don't want to hurt you. It's all down to circumstance. Come on, tell me."

The very idea of bishops triggered in Julian the memory of their last showdown and the way they had looked at him. Their scorn had crushed him. For the bishops, sending Julian Crabbe to Stickle was about as bad as a penance comes in the Church of England. It was like being cast into the wilderness, and it did start that way and that was what it was for the first few months. Now he didn't want to be sent away again, sent somewhere horrible, somewhere where things he couldn't deal with were constantly being asked of him. Stickle was home now, and more, he loved Penelope. He wanted to be left alone with his dying congregation; he wanted, if there was a God, to love it in his own way. He wanted to express love through Penelope and through all the little things he did every day, to be near to real life and to love.

Like a good man of violence, Carter could read almost every skittering emotion on the vicar's face, knew when to tighten his grip, when to relax it. The need to talk was in Julian's pleading eyes, and Carter gave it air, just enough. Almost despite himself, with the first taste of vomit in the back of his throat, the vicar choked out, "D.C."

It was a word—no, it was less than a word, it was two letters—and Carter retightened his grip on the vicar's throat, while he tried to understand the meaning and turn it to his advantage. It was the game. D.C. It was a name. He needed more. Time to be nice. With a soft smile, Carter lowered the vicar's feet to the floor and, releasing his grip, straightened Julian's dog collar, patted his shoulder, and said, "Now that wasn't too hard, was it?"

All restrictions gone, Julian Crabbe's face lengthened and distorted and, like a silent scream, a mini–tidal wave of puke forced its way past his teeth. It wasn't exactly slo-mo, but Carter could almost see it coming. He sprang back and managed to dodge the worst but just wasn't quick enough. A violent splurt of chrome-yellow vomit splashed down the front of his suit jacket.

For a moment, Carter was stunned. It was like a violation, a finger poked in the ever-open wound of his childhood, but he wasn't a child anymore in worn-out clothes he didn't want to wear and getting a bath only once a week. That was long ago, in times he didn't want to think about. These days he kept himself neat, clean; it was an ethos from his teen years. Clean living in difficult circumstances.

Carter didn't like the past. Carter went mad. He couldn't stop himself. With a scream, he threw the vicar down onto the lino and pinned him with his knees. Carter raised his arms above his head and balled his two fists together. He was going to smash this fucker's face.

Simp heard the scream. He got up from the table and went through to the kitchen. He grabbed Carter's upraised fists in one hand and put his other arm around his boss's chest and pulled him kicking and cursing off the vicar. For a few moments Simp held him, like a mother holds a child, and crooned, over and over, "Leave it, boss, it's not worth it." He gave Carter two of his tablets.

From his prone position, Julian Crabbe watched the tableau of the two men. He didn't understand it, but then he didn't understand anything very much. He figured, if you didn't know what was going on, it was probably best to keep quiet. He'd read a book once by Franz Kafka, where a man wakes up and he'd been turned into a beetle. He felt like an upturned beetle now, or a crab, in name and perhaps nature. *Show me my rock to crawl under, please.* And like the chap in the book, he didn't understand what was happening. He was scared. He didn't know what to do, so he simply stayed where he was.

When Carter had calmed down, Simp left him standing like a five-year-old in a corner and went over to help Julian Crabbe back onto his feet. It was cleanup time. There wasn't much Simp could say. You couldn't explain Carter to anyone. He said, "I don't know what happened here. The boss is usually such a gentle man." Julian began to tell him but Simp held up a hand. He didn't have the words to explain and he didn't want to hear. Julian dusted himself down and tried again, but Simp wouldn't let him. Instead he gripped the top of the vicar's arm and, taking the wrist with the watch on it in the other hand, turned it, checked the time, and said, "Time's flying by. Your pensioners will be here in fifteen minutes."

Julian looked at Simp goggle-eyed. Who were these people? What had he done, what had he said? D.C. He started to stutter, to try to take it back, but Simp tightened his grip and gently tugged him across the room.

To Julian, Carter looked like someone on heavy medication, which he was. Eyes like big blue saucers, his two hands held up limply, like a kangaroo's in a boxing ring. His nose twitched.

Simp said, "Look at him. Look at how upset he is."

No. To Julian he looked mad.

To Carter, Simp said, "Don't worry, boss, everything's all right. The vicar here is a very reasonable man." Carefully Simp slipped a hand into Carter's jacket pocket and took out a wallet. "I'm just going to give the rev a few bob for his trouble, all right?"

Carter seemed to refocus. He looked from Simp to Julian, back to Simp, and nodded slowly.

The wallet was fat and Simp opened it. There was more money than Julian had seen in a long time. Simp took five twenty-pound notes and spread them in a fan. Julian was weak. He took the money and toddled off toward his elderly parishioners and their coffee, even though he didn't like what had happened. He knew it wasn't right. He knew he needed moral guidance. He knew he needed to talk to Postmistress P. Nevertheless, he resolved to go first to see the old dears and geezers, to look after them, to smile and give them the buns, scones, tea cakes, tea, and coffee they had supplied. All Julian ever did was act like a friendly waiter, going from person to person, feeding and watering them and listening to what they had to say about their swollen ankles and dicky hearts, their personal gripes and little triumphs. He knew them all and they were his work, his parishioners, and he even liked some them, but most of all, he wanted to lie in the comfort of his lover's arms.

Using the washing-up water and the dishcloth, Simp cleaned the puke off Carter's jacket as best he could. The two men didn't talk. Simp had been here before and now sometimes it was too much. Often it was too much. These days he looked about at other people, at their lives, and how times had changed, and he wondered if he could ever have another life and what form that life would take. While he scrubbed, Simp watched as Carter paced back and forth across the room. He could see by the way Carter moved that he was trying to give it, to get the attitude back, but to Simp, Carter looked like a subdued version of himself. *Smaller* wouldn't be the right word to use, and everybody has triggers. Everybody is sensitive. The past bites everybody on the arse at some time.

15

As usual, that morning, the inhabitants of Stickle Island went about their business, which wasn't much, and they did it under soft blue skies. Stickle in June was all sweet and dandy, smelling of blossom and brine, and green for the eyes everywhere and all the birds singing.

Early, because of his nature, D.C. went to the beach as usual, but he wasn't really looking for firewood. Instead he mooched up and down, thinking. Although D.C. was a Petal pushover, he was worried. With around two million quid in contention, nothing was fixed, and people mostly saw pound notes, so there was a chance she would have a job bringing the whole island with her, and not just because of the money. He knew a lot of people—sensible, intelligent people—were against drugs.

On the rest of the island, all the old-timers were up and ready to rock, early. The ones who could drive ferried the ones who couldn't, and they all brought their Tupperware containers chock-full of cakes and buns and sandwiches. They set up the Cona coffee machine and the tea urn. Everything was well under control even before the vicar arrived.

On their farm, the Newmans were about their business too, with cows and sheep and things like that. Later they went to the barn and Si showed his dad the bales of dope. They talked again about the meeting and then there were phone calls too, between Julie and John, and phone calls between Petal and Si, and phone calls between Petal and Dick.

In the meantime, between dawn and nine A.M., Postmistress P opened shop and was behind the counter, everything she should be. At the dock, kids caught the ferry to school, as kids should. Petal went over to Dymchurch at the same time and stood outside the library, waiting for it to open. By ten A.M., Julian Crabbe made an appearance for his elderly parishioners, rubbing his hands together and giving it his best shot despite everything and happy there was money in his pocket.

On the Sticks' farm a half dozen hands arrived and started the cleanup. Some slept in and turned up late, unconcerned. What was all the fuss about anyway? Nothing was happening now, the storm was over already! But they worked hard anyway, mostly for Dick. They re-staked the fruit bushes, picked and boxed everything that was salvageable. They cut away and began to replace the plastic sheeting on the ruined polytunnels. They hoed away at this and that and they were all good hoes. Sure, Henry Stick was about, like an overseer, but they all knew it was Dick who figured things out. He didn't quibble if they were late and he'd share a joint with them, and, better still, he paid their wages in cash, and if you were on the dole, as most were, *cash* was a good word. Everybody knew where they stood with cash.

Carter and Simp came out into this lovely world, and looking about, Carter said, "Whatever happens, we ain't missing that ferry this afternoon." Simp breathed deeply and took in the remains of the dew on the grass, the blackbird singing, and the fresh way the air shriveled his headache into nothing. In that morning, at that moment, Simp didn't care much about what Carter wanted or what there was to lose or gain. Seeing his boss earlier in the kitchen had sort of sickened him. He didn't mind violence—sometimes he even enjoyed it—but rage, uncontrollable rage, of the sort he'd seen over and over with Carter, he still didn't understand. The older he got the less he liked it, the less he wanted to deal with Carter's mental problems. Sometimes, these days, it seemed he was more carer than minder. Anyway, it was one thing dealing with people in the business, but these people, people like the vicar, were civilians. It didn't feel right. He'd go with Carter and do whatever needed to be done. He wouldn't like it, but your job's your job.

As they got in the car and tootled off, instead of thinking about what they were doing, Simp thought about being young, about when he'd been sent down to that farm because his mum was in the hospital. Happiness is a strange thing. For some, leaving his sick mother to live with strangers should have been heartrending, but, in fact, it had been the best summer of Simp's life. It was easy. People had liked him and had taken care of him, and although he didn't understand why, he'd fitted in. By the end of the summer, when his mother was already home convalescing, he didn't want to go home, and now, as he breathed in the morning air, he knew why. Somehow, suddenly, this Kent countryside felt more like home than South London.

He rolled down the window because a mild miasma of puke hung around Carter, plonked in the passenger seat. Not nice. It was obvious Carter could smell it too, but he just sat there, nose curling, building back his ego. Not really wanting to talk, Simp stuck a soul compilation into the tape deck. "The Tears of a Clown" came on, then "I Heard It Through the Grapevine"; next was "Me and Mrs. Jones."

In his seat, Carter rolled his shoulders, gave Simp a snide look, and sucked air through his teeth. "What a pathetic pair of tossers! Did you ever listen to the lyrics of this?"

Simp looked out the open window at the passing hedge-row.

"Listen. They meet every day at the same café. How fucking boring is that? Every day, and ooh, they both know it's wrong—fuck me, all they do is hold hands and listen to their favorite fucking song and go home! Oh no, right, I forgot, they meet same time, same place, the next fucking day. Exactly what is it they've got going on? Fuck all, if you ask me!"

Simp reached over and ran the tape on to the next song.

Carter said, "There's a bloke here called D.C., let's find him."

16

D.C. wasn't exactly surprised when the BMW stopped outside the gate to the field. He stopped chopping kindling and faced the two men, machete dangling loose in his hand. As they unhooked the field gate, he pointed the machete at them. "Close that."

Carter held up his hands and Simp, watching D.C. the whole time, pushed it shut and dropped the latch. Simp had met many D.C. types during his career, and they could be good, they could be dangerous, but violence was Simp's living, and although he may get hurt, this guy would be dead. He moved away from Carter's side and set himself at an angle to D.C.

As he watched the two men approach, D.C. backed off until he felt the sun-warmed aluminum of the trailer against his shoulder blades and managed to put the woodpile between himself and Carter. The big man was coming forward slowly. Blood was singing through D.C.'s veins, he glanced down at the machete in his hand and wondered what he really was. The way he saw it, there were people who saw everything as a tool and there were people who saw everything as a weapon. He'd tried to alter himself, tried to be different and was still trying. The two men attempted to stare him down, but it didn't happen. D.C. took a proper grip on the machete, and while waiting to take out the big man's ankles, he thought about his garden and the pig and how much he would miss making his own bread. He didn't need to kill anybody, just bring them down, but...

Simp came forward knowing the machete was his. It would come at him and only the moment was win or lose. Everything he'd ever done worked up through his blood and he waited in his mind somewhere else, like D.C. waited.

Carter was volatile, unpredictable, but he was also smart and had been a criminal all his life. Mostly he knew the time for violence and the time for talk, even if he hated it. So, holding his hands out, palms down, he pushed gently against the air as though testing the firmness of a mattress, and backing off a pace or two, he said, "Let's talk, you know, have a bit of a chat."

Simp was a lump of a man and he made it crowded in the trailer. He perched his arse on the edge of the unlit wood-burning stove and was quiet, but he took up space. If he stretched his arms, he could easily punch out all the windows. He listened.

The first thing D.C. said to Carter was "You've got puke down the front of your suit."

Simp stifled a laugh as Carter stiffened but managed, unusually, to keep his temper. His pills were working. They talked, but bets were hedged. D.C. made tea and threw a few of last year's magic mushrooms into the pot, just to soften the edges. Nothing got resolved. Both men knew what was being talked about. They drank tea. Things went around and around. D.C. didn't own up to knowing where the bales were; instead he told them to look about outside. He said, "If the bales are there you can have them." He watched through the window as they slowly scouted the perimeter of the field, poked in the ditches, checked out the henhouse, and searched under the trailer. When they returned, D.C. poured more tea.

In most cross-party discussions, the party of desperation gives in first because it has the most to lose, and so it was with Carter. Carter told D.C. his little story about the weather and loss of income and indicated how the situation could be resolved easily with or without violence and waved the back of his hand at Simp. "Hours he was, walking up and down that desolate beach!" He raised his shoulders and opened the palms of his hands at D.C. "Look at him, barely half the man he was!"

D.C. smiled. Simp shrugged.

Carter said, "Okay, maybe we got off to a bad start, but honest, we don't want any trouble, I just want my product back."

Downing his tea in a gulp, Simp took another refill and stepped outside again. He didn't need to hear any more. Simp knew it was all bullshit. Whatever was agreed to now wouldn't matter on the day. The bales were Carter's and he was going to take them back.

For a while, all was quiet between the two men, until D.C. said, "So how much would you give to get those bales back?"

Carter looked around the trailer. It was fucking pathetic how some people were prepared to live, like that fucking vicar with his kitchen from the Dark Ages. *Leave me out.* It was hard to keep the contempt from his voice but he thought he managed. "Well, let's say I'd be more than generous. How would ten thousand pounds sound to you?"

They looked at each other and drank their tea. D.C. refilled the cups, and they drank. He said, "I ain't no quantity surveyor, but my guess is that little lot has got to be worth at least like two million quid."

Carter couldn't argue. It was near enough, but he was losing patience and it went against the grain to negotiate. He thought, *Fuck you, we'll just come back and take it.* Then, almost without him noticing, a gentle wave rolled through his system, and despite himself, he said, "All right, twenty."

D.C. watched Carter. He said, "I think ten percent would be more like it. About two hundred thousand pounds."

That brought Carter back to earth. Money always sharpened his senses. He laughed. It wasn't a very nice laugh. "You're out of your league."

D.C. smiled. "Am I?"

With a shake of his head, Carter said, "What do you do, eh? A few quarters, bits and bobs. You think you know but you don't understand the game." Maybe he would have said more or threatened more, but the mushrooms came on him again.

D.C. could see it, and he said, "Don't I? I was born game. Look, you're a villain, so your game is fixed because you think yours is the only game, and that's a weakness. On the other hand, you don't know me and you don't know my game. True, you may know your own environment, but this ain't your environment, old son. You don't know the people living on this island and that could prove a mistake."

Carter didn't really listen to a word D.C. said. Instead he watched the way the light fell through the dirty window and across the tabletop and the way it made the tiny little bits of silvery stuff in the Formica sparkle, and he thought of his daughter, Amber, and her refusal to go back to school. Yeh, he'd spoiled her, and now he didn't know what to do with her. Under his breath he mumbled, "She's a good girl really."

Time passed. Simp opened the trailer door and looked about. The inside was all roundy and kind of pink and homely, and someone had brightened it up while he'd been talking to the pig. He looked at D.C. and D.C. was smiling, and all he could do was smile back. Everything went flat for a moment. Reality checkpoint. Talking to the pig? He reached in the door and tugged at Carter's sleeve. It wasn't that he was paranoid, but something wasn't right. "I think we should go, boss."

They left like children, nothing resolved.

After they'd gone, D.C. took a flagon of island cider from the fridge, poured a glass, and rolled a joint, and everything was lovely, so he carried a chair outside and sat propped back against the trailer in the sun and watched his pig root around in its enclosure, listened to the birds sing, and loved life and the earth he lived on.

17

That morning, when Petal awoke in her bed, her first unbidden thought was of Si and how their legs had touched when they were taking the bales up to the barn, and that made her think about when they were still both children, always running around together, her, Si, and Dick, always together. The second unbidden thought was how Si and she had practiced kissing, silly kids' stuff, way, way before she'd thought about boyfriends. As he'd grown older, the scant years between them seemed to stretch, and Si had become shyer and she knew, even if she hadn't gone with Dick, she could have died of old age before Si made a move. Now she wasn't so sure. It felt like something between them was different. The last of the unbidden thoughts came as understanding. It was like, until the previous day, she'd grown into the habit of seeing Si merely as a friend. He'd always been there, but now she didn't know how things had changed or how quickly. In the warmth of the bed, her body had its own kind of fuzzy logic, and she tried to think of Dick, but Si wouldn't go away. It was that touching in the tractor. Leg against leg. That moment when skin becomes electric. She knew it but didn't want to fully acknowledge it.

When Petal came down, Julie was already up drinking tea. Petal made toast. They talked about this and that, the way people who live together do, and they talked about the bales and what to do next. Although Petal wouldn't admit the fact to anyone, even to her ever-loving mum, she knew jack shit about co-ops. She kind of knew what a co-op was but not how to start one. Her mind oscillated between that and Si and Dick. She drank her tea, mind still half under the bedclothes, and sulked and sighed and ate her toast and needed a little help but didn't want to ask for it. She drank more tea and tossed the crust of her toast back onto the plate, sniffed and held her head in her hands, and said, "Shit, what am I going to do?"

Julie wasn't an expert, but before they had moved, when they'd lived in the London squats, she'd been part of a food co-op. It had been a small affair, but Julie guessed the legal stuff would be more or less the same and Petal could probably find out most of what she needed to know when she went to the library. Petal grimaced at the term *legal*. Julie patted her daughter's knee. "From what I remember it's all got to be quite businesslike, and before a meeting can take place there has to be a quorum."

Petal laughed. "What's a quorum?"

Unable to exactly remember, Julie got the dictionary and thumbed through it. She said, "Apparently, it's like the amount of members required before any business can be transacted."

At a loss, Petal yeh-yeh'd her mother. There was too much to think about. She wanted to get things started, if only to distract herself. Si kept drifting into her mind. Right or wrong, something needed to happen. She pulled on a jumper and headed to the ferry, leaving her mother to arrange the meeting. Julie phoned John Newman about having it at his place later that night, and John, in turn, called on D.C. to pass along the information.

The two men sat and watched the pig root around in its sty. They drank cold cider. After a while, D.C. asked, "So did you meet our visitors?"

John shook his head. "No. Si told me he'd seen some strangers. They stayed at the rectory, right?"

D.C. nodded. "I reckon. But anyway, that stuff in your barn, it's theirs."

Taking a deep breath, Newman sighed. "What did they want?"

D.C. shook his head. "Leave out that naive shit, John. They want it back, what else?"

With a swig of cider, Newman grunted amiably. "What did you tell them?"

"Well, I told them we would want about ten percent of value. The main man didn't like that." He paused. "Oh yeh, and I put mushrooms in their tea."

John Newman started to chuckle and then D.C. too. After a little while, John said, "That must have helped."

Innocent as, D.C. laughed again. "Don't know really. When the mushies came on they left in a bit of a hurry."

Glass out for more, Newman said, "I wonder what they did. It's one of those times, you know, you'd just like to watch. To be there, like the ghost in that *Ghost and Mrs. Muir*. Do you think they were all right?"

D.C. wished with all his heart he'd never have to see Carter or Simp again. He wished the mushrooms he'd given them had sent the pair of them stark staring mad and that they'd been taken off the ferry in an ambulance to a nuthouse, destination unknown. Never to be seen again. Fuck them!

He said, "Sure, they'll have been all right for a few hours, but when they come down they'll be the same pair of cunts they always were. Some people are just built like that. Anyway, who cares, they caught the ferry, I saw them." They drank. D.C. said, "But, John, they'll be coming back for sure. These two, they ain't no mugs, and it could get nasty. We'll have to think about that."

Quaker and pacifist blood still dribbled through John Newman's veins, and diluted as it was, he still didn't like trouble, he didn't like violence, and he didn't like the sound of dealing with a bunch of villains. What if they came back and took what they wanted? How could they stop them?

D.C. shook his head. "I don't know, it could be we'll be hurt. Me, I don't care, I'll take my chances, but don't know about everybody else."

Even John understood he wouldn't be able to pacify his way out of that kind of violence. Money. He didn't like it but knew it was all about money. There was no meaning. Bought and sold was all most folks ever were. Over and over. Democracy was a con, a kind of volunteer slavery. Newman swallowed the rest of his cider and rose to leave. He stretched but said nothing because he didn't know what to say.

D.C. said, "Don't worry." Then he smiled all inscrutable-like. "Eight's fine with me but I'm bringing one more person along."

John Newman sighed, shrugged. "Who?"

All enigmatic, D.C. tapped the side of his nose. "I know one thing for sure, this ain't going to happen without him."

18

Earlier, after Carter and Simp left the trailer, they almost began to drive away, but the world was strange. They looked at each other boggle-eyed, giggle giddy, daft as brushes. Laughing, Carter said, "Wow! What do you think was in that tea?"

Simp smiled sloppily. "Don't know, boss, but whatever it was, it works."

Carter watched Simp attempting to fit the key into the car's ignition and asked, "Do you think you can drive?"

What the fuck did Simp know? He giggled. "If I can get the key in the ignition, we'll give it a go, eh?"

They started laughing again, and suddenly the key fit in the hole and it was tight like that, and Simp thought of the dead blues singer Clara Smith and then thousands upon thousands of automatic physical responses, compounded day in and day out, kicked in, and like he was normal, Simp turned the key and watched as, on the dash, all the little lights started shining, and he thought of Joni Mitchell. He couldn't hear the engine and the steering wheel seemed soft and malleable, but, eyes wide, he did what drivers do next and put the BMW in gear. The clutch, brake, and accelerator were like small, live animals tickling his toes through the soles of his trainers. He didn't feel dangerous, he felt sensitive. He drove carefully.

For reasons Carter couldn't be bothered to understand, he was excessively happy. The world was melting around him and he didn't care. Everything made him want to laugh and that was such an unusual and good feeling that he couldn't help but give vent to his joy. In a wavering but tuneful voice, he started to sing a Small Faces song: *"Here come the nice, looking so good, he makes me feel like no one else could."*

They tootled along. Sometimes the hedgerow was a continuous sunny glade with a twisty little tarmac path that they followed like a pair of little red hooting rides, and other times they watched the rise and fall of the road like they were on a river spreading out wide as it flowed between super-green hedgerows and big open fields dotted with some kind of black-and-white bovines of a caliber they had never seen before. More surreal than Milton Keynes concrete cows—no, not happening. They marveled momentarily. Then there was something else.

They had no real idea where they drove or for how long, but almost unconsciously, like homing pigeons, they found themselves once again at Fishtail Bay. They wandered about on the beach, sat and marveled at empty shells and sea-worn colored stones, at the movement of the sea, at the wheeling sea birds, happy out.

Out of the blue, Carter said, "I wish I had a fishing rod. I'd just like to sit out on those rocks there and do nothing, never again. Catch a fish, fry it, throw out the line. Simple as that."

The ridiculousness of Carter doing nothing broke Simp up, and the state of Simp broke Carter up, and when they'd recovered, they gave each other man hugs like a couple of hippie twats.

Hours went by, and when normality slowly returned, they went to the dock and waited, docile-like, for the ferry. Simp said, "I like it here."

Carter, slipping back into reality, said, "If you like it so much, why don't you move down here and become a carrot cruncher, grow your hair, buy a checked shirt, and start listening to country and fucking western music, instead of that soul crap you like so much."

Still with a little edge of mushrooms on him, Simp looked about and said, "Yeh, maybe I will."

19

The first meeting wasn't called to order, they didn't elect a chair, no one cared about a quorum, a secretary wasn't appointed, and no one took notes.

John Newman and Si, Julie, Petal, and Dick were already sitting at the big deal table in the Newmans' kitchen with mugs of tea in their hands, chatting as they waited. When D.C. walked in with PC Paloney, the talking stopped. Mouths hung open, stalled in midsentence. Mugs hung dangerously, halfway between lip and sip. They all became quiet. With a grin, D.C. put an arm around Paloney's shoulders. "This is my mate Phil."

The silence hung. D.C. hugging the policeman was an unexpected occurrence. Eyes skittered as thoughts of prison flickered through their minds. D.C. looked quizzically from person to person.

"What's up, ain't you ever seen a pig out of its official blanket before? Look, he knows everything. He watched us taking the stuff off the beach. He's here to help and we'll need him on our side if this is going to work." He paused and rubbed his hands together. "Now, how about a cup of tea?"

While he waited for tea to be poured, D.C. explained about Paloney, and Paloney explained about himself and how he didn't want the island to become a drugs staging post, but on the other hand he really liked living on the island and he didn't want the place shut down by a bunch of bureaucrats.

Talk turned to the intentions of the two strangers who'd come to the island. John Newman pointed to D.C. as the only person who'd had any actual contact and Paloney added, "Apart from the vicar and the postmistress. I'll call there tomorrow and see what they made of them."

D.C. told what he knew. These were frightening, dangerous people, and if the island was going to do something collectively, they better get it together quickly and be ready. It could turn nasty. When Julie suggested that maybe, as they didn't know exactly where the dope was, they would give it up and not bother to come back, D.C. smiled. Julie had a kind and loving heart and always looked at life in that way, despite knockbacks, and that was nice, but then again, she hadn't run into Simp and Carter, he had.

He said, "They know it's here, not exactly where but they know, and they'll be back all right and bloody soon." He rubbed his thumb and forefinger together. "Money. That lot in the barn has got to be worth about two million. It's not grass they see, it's money. Look, we'll have to be ready for them; these aren't your average businessmen."

There was a silence while the rest of them around the table considered consequences and their own fearful hearts. Julie asked, "How much are we talking about?"

"The smaller guy offered ten grand," D.C. replied. "More when the mushrooms got him, but I wouldn't rely on that."

A light went on in most people's eyes. Fist clenched, Petal said, "Brill'!"

With a withering look at his daughter, D.C. added, "I told them we'd want somewhere in the region of two hundred thousand pounds."

Si whistled quietly. "That's an awful lot of money. Don't get me wrong, I think Petal's idea is great, but a lot of people would kill for that much money."

With a sniff, D.C. shot a sideways glance at Petal. "Well, let's face it, you can't change fuck all with ten grand. Seems to me we'll have to fight to get what we want."

It was a horrible truth and everyone sat in silence. They could all see perhaps ten grand could change something on a personal level, but spread over the island it would be scrape thin.

Phil Paloney spoke first. "However much money is involved, I think D.C.'s right. If they come back we'll have to be ready for them."

Petal could feel the surreptitious, gentle pressure of Si's knee as it rested against hers. Regardless of whether their legs had touched by chance or design, neither moved. What happens under the table stays under the table, but no—what was happening under the table was affecting her whole body and quite a bit of her mind. She was all over the place. What was actually happening, like having a policeman in on it all and hearing him and her dad agree, was just a bit weird. And the amount of cash involved seemed huge, much more than she'd imagined. Now there was the fear of what could happen if it went wrong. And the slap down from D.C. hurt; he knew how to get her.

At the library, she'd had no trouble finding the right book *A Modern Guide to Forming a Co-op*—but it had been in the reference section and could not be borrowed. She'd scanned through it, trying as best she could to pick out the relevant bits, but it hadn't been easy, beginning with the fact that there were several types of co-ops, depending on how it was financed and how the members expected the co-op to function. The members, which in Stickle's case would be everybody living on the island, had to agree and adopt a governing document. Just the idea of Stickle people all agreeing was mind-boggling, never mind the legalese, much of which she didn't understand. Nevertheless, she'd photocopied a dozen or so pages, which she intended to study until she did understand. The trouble was, by the time she was back on Stickle, the meeting had been arranged and she hadn't had time to absorb any of it. Then there was Si and Dick, and she just wasn't prepared.

Everything seemed changed and a bit out of control, and somehow her throat was dry and she realized she was holding her breath. The idea of dealing with actual criminals hadn't occurred to Petal before, and being ready for them—what did that mean? Would they have to fight them? What if innocent islanders were hurt? She couldn't think straight. It was like too much information! And then, of course, Dick was sitting beside her on the other side, one hand resting on her thigh and with absolutely no idea what she was feeling. It was overload—her heart was beating *bish, bash, bosh*—and also, she had gone partially deaf. She just couldn't concentrate or seem to grasp what was being said. People spoke but their words flew past her ears and out the door, gone forever. And still she left her knee where it was, against Si's.

Stuff was talked about and she heard words and even whole sentences without connecting one to another. Sometimes she breathed and sometimes she held her breath back. The feelings she was feeling moved almost too quickly. It was like the Si thing had come up all of a sudden and slapped her. The fact it was someone she'd known since childhood seemed to make things stranger. What had changed? Something about Si and his thigh against hers. She liked it; it wasn't his fault. Dick, on the other hand, hand on her thigh, she didn't know now about him anymore. What had changed? She didn't know. She couldn't think. What was that white noise? Then suddenly it seemed Dick was talking and that was unusual. Mostly he left the talking to her.

Dick said, "I know you're talking about doing something for the whole island and all that, but what if some people don't agree? What if they just want to take their share of the money and leave?"

Petal tried to focus. Dick's hand wasn't touching her thigh anymore. Instead, Dick was gesturing about above the table, like he had a point to make. Petal gaped at him. The money was for the island and the people of the island. It wasn't a personal thing; it was a communal thing. Why would anybody want to take money that was never even theirs? She tried to protest.

Dick laughed. "If someone offered me ten grand or something, I'd leave like a shot!"

Petal looked disbelievingly at her boyfriend. Was he serious? Ever since he'd gone to see his mother, he'd talked about leaving the island and going to London, but Petal had shrugged it off as just talk, but maybe there was more to it than that.

Dick's mother had run off back to London when he was in the terrible twos, and he'd not seen her again until earlier this year. Apparently, she had offered him a room in her house. What was that about? They hardly knew each other. Dick had talked about them going away together, but Petal wasn't going anywhere. She'd been born in London and that was enough already!

Meeting his mother after so many years had changed a few things for Dick. He couldn't help but blame his father for keeping them apart all these years, but Henry was old and he'd had a hard life, and like most men of a certain age, he was an emotional cripple. But what was hard had become harder recently, as he'd realized his father could no longer run the farm without him. That scared him. He had ideas and ambitions and felt hamstrung by his father, the island, and Petal was great but...

Everyone assumed he didn't know his mother and that was true, but she had, all through his childhood, sent birthday and Christmas presents. A return address was never included. Then, on his eighteenth birthday, a check had arrived and a letter with her address. She hadn't said sorry or anything like that, but like the past was the past, right?

It had taken close on two years for Dick to pluck up the courage to go and see her. Even then his dad didn't like it, but what could he do? She'd invited Dick to visit and that was what he'd done, and, yes, his mother had offered him a place to stay, but his father was an obligation he didn't know how to get out of. He'd raised him despite everything, and you can't dodge that bullet. If anybody ever wanted a prodigal brother to turn up out of the blue, it was Dick. Yes, kill the fatted calf and then he, Dick, could just bugger off. He knew it wasn't going to happen. There wasn't a long-lost brother, sister, auntie, uncle, cousin, no one. They were the last of the line.

"Dipstick's got a point, but we can sort that out later," D.C. said.

Dipstick! Petal's natural instinct was to jump and defend Dick, as she had so many times before, but the words stuck in her craw. She bit her lip and almost unconsciously let her hand slip from where it lay on the table until, beneath, it came to rest on Si's thigh. She felt him tense before his hand softly covered her own.

Across the table, John Newman said, "Yes, whatever about that. Come on, Petal, let's hear what you have to say."

They all looked at her. She realized she didn't know what she had to say anymore. They all waited on her. Petal had spent half the day thinking, but now her mind was a complete blank. She needed more time to study the co-op idea and form a proper plan. She tried to remember the passion she'd felt when she'd confronted D.C. on the beach and hoped that it could carry her through now, but with Dick on one side and

Si on the other, it was all getting too complicated. Then there were the dodgy fucks they had to deal with to make it happen, not to mention the amount of money D.C. had talked about. It all seemed like too much.

Removing her hand from beneath Si's, Petal got to her feet. Standing was a mistake. Looking down on those expectant faces, when she didn't have an idea: not good. Nothing was in her mind, and if any of them thought she had an original idea, could they please tell her what it was, right now? One of the things she'd learned from D.C. was to let them know: when you walk, you've got your head up, regardless, and when you've got nothing, go aggressive. She took a deep breath and said whatever came into her head. "What does it matter? What has it got to do with me? Everything I thought has been messed up already, with crime and money. I didn't know, I just thought we could save the island. Maybe we still could but I don't know how! All right, call me stupid, but I still think a co-op is a valid idea. I've been to Dymchurch and found out some stuff about co-ops but..." She stumbled and stuttered and came to a sliding halt. When she sat down, Si took one hand and, unbeknownst on the other side, Dick took the other, and that was all very well, but the other faces around the table told her the truth.

What she'd said was nonsense. She could feel the tears pricking at the back of her eyes, even before D.C. shook his head and said, "You've let me down. You know, I listened to you on the beach and I thought about what you said and I could see the sense in it. But you ain't convinced me this time, and if you can't convince me, don't know how you expect to convince the rest of the people when we get them together. You better think on and sort yourself out."

On the verge of tears, Petal looked at her dad, and harsh as he was, he was right but it didn't help.

Julie snapped, "D.C.!"

At the same moment, Si pushed back his chair and jumped to his feet. "That's not fair! The idea was Petal's but you can't expect her to think of everything!"

With a withering look, D.C. said, "An idea is just that, an idea. We all get them, it's what your brain's for. Ideas go nowhere unless you come up with the practicals. An idea is like philosophy, no use unless it works in everyday life. I'm telling you, when they come back these people won't come back with flowers in their hands." He pointed at Petal and shook his head. "I expect more of you, girl. If that's all you got, I'm off. Let me know when you've sorted yourself out." He turned and headed for the door.

Julie and Phil Paloney chorused, "D.C.!"

John Newman rose and followed him to the door. "Come on, D.C., we're here to sort this out between us. Don't go."

But D.C. wasn't listening. He waved a hand over his shoulder as he mounted his bike and said, "Talk to them about starting a co-op, John, that was one of Petal's original ideas that she seems to have forgotten about. If we manage to get the money, we've got to clean it—you can't just walk into a bank with that much cash and open an account. I'll see you, John Newman."

The meeting dissolved but not before John Newman had a say. If they could manage to sell it, without too much trouble, he wasn't against the idea of using the dope money to revitalize the island, but it couldn't stay in his barn, it was too easy to find. Lift up the tarpaulin and there it was. Julie told them she would help Petal with the co-op idea. As a group, they went and looked in the barn, and for those like Julie and Phil Paloney, who'd not seen it all together in a lump, as it were, there seemed to be an awful lot of it.

Back in the kitchen they thought about where it could be hidden. Dick suggested the police house. Ho fucking ho!

Paloney put the blocks on that. There was a derelict just outside the village—an option perhaps. Trouble was then anybody could find it. Underground would have been ideal, but there weren't any caves on Stickle. No! It was Kent, not Derbyshire. Bury it? That would need to be quite a big hole. Some of the other blow-ins who liked a smoke had sheds and garages where it could be hidden, but then that was just more people to deal with, more chances of chat. More chances for things to go wrong.

They thought and pondered, and then Si looked at Dick and said, "What about those old cellars under your house? No one goes there. In fact most people don't even know they exist. Reckon it would be safe there, wouldn't it?"

The cellars! Dick shook his head. "What about my dad? He'd go mad if he found out!"

Si said, "Come on, your dad wouldn't even know—I bet he never goes down there."

Dick was in a corner. He looked around the table. They were all waiting.

In the end, he swallowed and mumbled, "Well, he's going over to Dymchurch Friday for glass for the greenhouses. When he goes, he usually stays and comes back on the Saturday afternoon ferry."

With uncharacteristic finality, Si smiled. "So we do it Friday after the ferry leaves."

20

It was about eight A.M. when D.C. arrived at Julie's the next morning. "I came to say sorry to Petal, maybe help her," he said, and shrugged. "You know, get a proper plan together before the next meeting."

Julie tilted her head and scowled. There was more than one reason she wasn't happy to see her ex-husband so early in the morning, and she said, "The thing I've always liked about you, D.C., is you're always yourself."

D.C. puffed his chest out and grinned happily. "That's what I try to be—"

But Julie cut him short with a look. She didn't need to hear how it was basic existential philosophy, how it was important to be in the moment whenever possible. All she could see at that moment was the little-girl-lost look on Petal's face as he'd left the meeting the previous night.

With an edge, Julie said, "Sometimes, in certain circumstances, I wish you could be someone else instead. Just for a few minutes, you know?" Julie always knew how and when she'd hurt D.C. If he loved you, it was easy, and now she could see the little movements of despair all across his features. She didn't want to hurt him, but there it was. Love is a strange thing. She watched the air come slowly out of D.C.'s lungs as he deflated and flopped down onto the couch. She sat on the couch arm and rested a hand on his knee.

Despite their differences, the pair generally supported each other, even occasionally still falling in bed together. But that wasn't now. Still with a chill, she said, "I know, I know, you don't want to hear it, but sometimes less is more. Sometimes your strength, it's like a weakness because it's unnecessary. You made Petal look like a fool. What did that achieve? What good did it do?"

For once D.C. didn't have a word to say. He knew she was right but it didn't stop him from hurting. He felt a great need to be comforted. There wasn't going to be any comfort. Hesitantly, he tried again: "I didn't—"

With a curt shake of her head, Julie stood and moved over to the sink. "Don't bother. I've known you for too long."

There were a few bits of dirty crockery in the washing-up bowl. Julie ran water. A squirt of liquid. With a cup and dishcloth in her hands, she paused and looked out across the field, where the chimney of the Newmans' farmhouse could be seen through the trees.

The floorboards creaked overhead and D.C. looked up. "Look, when she comes down I'll say sorry. I'll help her."

With a sigh, Julie let her hands dangle in the water, looked down, and closed her eyes. There was nothing she could do.

People expect to see what they expect to see. D.C. expected to see Petal. But it wasn't Petal coming down from above but John Newman. John Newman was a surprise. Something was wrong. D.C.'s brain demanded a moment, a hiatus, a time-out, as it tried to compute the bloody obvious. John Newman. Julie. Rewind. John Newman had just come downstairs. John Newman was hanging about first thing in the morning in his ex-wife's house. What's worse was that D.C. really liked John Newman. Worse yet, he still loved Julie. Why hadn't they told him?

Bolting upright and off the couch in a moment, D.C. strode, shoulders squared, two steps toward John. He shook his head and jabbed his finger, head all over the place. First time? No. He could tell. And if Petal knew, then Dipstick knew. And Si. For once he couldn't think of anything to say but continued to jab his finger at John anyway. He felt like a dill and turned away, walking back across the room, everything nagging at him now. Every moment was a moment to D.C., that was the way he tried to live. What a joke! Reality hurt. They had always pretended to be so grown-up about this sort of thing, and now he didn't feel very grown-up at all. They'd both had dalliances but had always kept it out of each other's faces. But this was John Fucking Newman. This was on another level.

Some things are going to come and come straight off, like a slap in the face; other things are on the horizon and come slowly, like the beast slouching toward Bethlehem, and John Newman had seen this coming a long way off, coming on slow, but now it was here and it was as it had always been, inevitable. The finger jabbing didn't bother him. He smiled, he said, "All right, D.C.?"

D.C. couldn't help himself. Didn't even ask himself. His voice was back. "What the fuck are you doing here at this time of fucking day! This is definitely going beyond the beyonce! Ain't you got some kind of bovine or ovine to castrate or some other farmyard shit to do?! Look at you, the fucking gay Lothario farmer sneaking down the stairs! Or is it just the landlord collecting his rent?"

Julie made to speak then, but before she could, John interrupted. "What? What are you on about? I've heard of 'begin the beguine,' but 'beyond the beyonce,' that's nonsense, even for you!" John Newman didn't like to argue but he didn't roll over either. Quietly, he added, "Sod you, old son."

D.C. shouted out that it was an old Battersea saying and something his old mother would say instead of swearing because she—unlike you, you cunt—was a very religious woman. D.C.'s raised voice brought Petal down from above, and she stood in the doorway at the foot of the stairs and watched.

John said some things, reasonable things, like "You told me you didn't know your parents. Foster homes and orphanages, wasn't it?" D.C. said things, unreasonable things, in an attempt to defend a mother he never knew, never had, and to slag off John.

At the sink Julie slapped her hand down hard on the draining board. "Stop it, D.C.! John and I, we—" She stopped. What was the point? She felt no reason to explain herself to him. She was a grown and independent woman, and he was like a child sometimes. Anyway, turn up uninvited and you find what you find. Herself and John had been seeing each other for nearly eighteen months. She sighed—maybe they should have told him at the start.

D.C. took the sigh as a sign he was off the hook and made to start up again, and Julie snapped, "Shut up! Just shut up!"

In the lull that followed, Petal said cheerily to John, "Call him a hippie."

D.C. sneered, John laughed, Julie laughed, Petal grinned. John Newman said, cheekily, "Don't come preaching morals to me, you old hippie!"

That was it. With nose-curling disgust, D.C. spat, "I ain't no fucking hippie! I never was! It's a fuck-off weak philosophy— all that 'we're all in it together' nonsense. It's patently fucking obvious we ain't, are we? Some people are takers. I don't know if it's genetic or what, but there ain't no changing the takers."

Newman frowned. He was getting a bit umpty himself now. D.C. lived free on his land. Had for years now. "Are you talking to me? Are you talking to me? Are you of all people calling me a taker?"

Defensive and wrong, again D.C. sneered like a child. "Fuck you! Take it however you like it. It's bad enough you sleep with my woman—"

The wet dishcloth flew across the kitchen and slapped D.C. upside the head. Without even looking at Julie, he picked it up from the floor where it had fallen, wiped the side of his face with his shirt cuff, and tossed it back into the sink.

"Okay! Sleep with my ex-wife. But I tell you, calling me a hippie, there you really insult me, John Newman." It was nonsense and he knew it.

They were all looking at him. Physically it was all there—the jabbing finger, the strutting shoulders—but the voice was weak. The power was gone. The argument was gone. D.C. was hurt and couldn't hide it. His Julie and John. He looked shocked, shook, the hard exterior beginning to crack and crumble, but luckily the foundations were deep and he held himself tight, despite the tears in his eyes. And, because there was still something between them, sometimes Julie thought to reach out to him but couldn't; she was just too angry. Instead she snapped again, "Get out!"

21

Meanwhile, Henry Stick looked down from his bedroom window at the back of the house as Dick pulled away the ivy, strung like a curtain down the walls and over the high old cellar doors. Henry Stick loved his son. He'd spent years bringing him up. That was more free love than anyone else had ever had from him. All right, he had to admit, sometimes he hadn't been perfect, but under his bluster, Dick was the one person who'd made his life bearable over the years. His boy. Wouldn't be worth the bother otherwise. No point otherwise. Was there really no future, like that song by the band Dick liked so much? Henry knew Dick didn't understand, didn't know, that despite the way things looked, he'd always tried to do his best.

What remained after the hurt of Sylvie leaving had gone, after all the years, was a sense of mistrust so deep and profound it had hampered his whole life. What did he have? Who were his friends? Who loved him? Life was pretty empty when he looked about. What Henry knew was you can't hold on to anything. It was all a matter of timing, and Henry understood that he was on the way to losing his son. The fact that he'd been to see his mother had complicated things, made it all stranger. Still, there was nothing to do but let things take their own course. He'd kept them apart since she'd left, but even he knew that hadn't been right. Just his cussedness. It was all over now, though. Worse now, now he'd been to see her. Things were coming to the surface. It was only a matter of time. He wanted to tell Dick everything: how she'd left like a thief in the night and how his once best friend had let her stay without even telling him. It was a rift between John Newman and himself that had never been resolved.

Below, Dick was scraping the vegetation he'd pulled from the wall away into a heap. Nobody ever went to the old cellars anymore. Sure, like Dick and Si, Henry had played down there when he was a young chavvy, playing cowboys with John in its half-dark world. A lifetime away. Sometimes he wished he could heal the rift between himself and John Newman, but it had gone on too long and he didn't know how to start. He pushed open the window and shouted, "What the hell you doing down there, you dozy git! Haven't you got enough to do without this? That bloody ivy takes years to grow and you get rid of it, just like that!"

Dick looked up at his father, hanging half out the window. His father pained him. He watched his friends with their parents, sometimes wanting whatever it was they had. But he didn't really know what it was they had and would never know. Casual as, he said, "I just thought I'd try and tidy the place up a bit."

Henry waved a hand about as though it had meaning. "Tidy up! I'd have thought there was plenty to do after the winds, and have you checked out those bloody hippie workers? What are they doing? Have they all turned up today?"

Dick picked up a tin of WD-40. "Why don't you go down and check? If you try hard enough I'm sure you can annoy them so they all go home and nothing gets done. Just leave it to me."

Dick squirted the WD-40 into the lock and down the heavy, old cast hinges. Henry watched him. He had his mother's looks, slim and handsome. Henry didn't want to look anymore. He shut the window. He hadn't a notion why his son was oiling the lock and hinges. Half rising, he thought about asking Dick but instead sat back down and began to pull on his boots. He'd take a look around, keep them useless casuals on their toes, measure up for the replacement glass. Maybe Dick was going to start a mushroom farm. He'd talked about that once. Commercial mushroom wrangling. *There* was a good market.

Later, Paloney went to see Postmistress P and found Julian Crabbe buying tinned pears, tinned pineapple chunks, and cling peaches, and Paloney wondered, *What are cling peaches anyway?* To Paloney's eye, Julian Crabbe was a trifle red-faced, and behind the counter Postmistress P looked particularly severe. It wasn't in his remit to interfere in what people called their personal life, their peccadilloes or whatever. He smiled at them and held his helmet in his hands.

After whatever years on the island, he'd got to know his own shortcomings quite well and almost everybody else's too. Which was unfortunate. He'd had to cultivate a blind side, like anybody who lives in a small community must develop a blind side and sometimes a deaf side. Paloney could see that Julian's fly was only half up, the zip caught in the tail of his shirt. Paloney said nothing.

Then he said, "You remember those two men? You know, the ones in the car? Did they stay with you, Julian, is that right?" Paloney studied the vicar and he was easy to see—almost everything he did was easy to see, written in every move and every gesture, every little facial tic—and it was obvious the vicar, Mr. Julian Crabbe, was a man who struggled with the concept of good and evil almost every day. His ability to believe in his chosen God often wavered, but good and evil were always manifest. He struggled. He struggled but his little pink cheeks and his zip at half-mast showed he didn't always win. Paloney didn't care.

Sticking up for her lover, Postmistress P said, "What would you expect a man of God to do? They had nowhere else to stay."

Paloney didn't care. He said, "I'm not here about anything, not really." He looked from face to face. Julian was all wide-eyed, like some kind of Bambi, caught in dangerous headlights. Postmistress P adjusted her glasses and, looking down, began to write in some ledger, cool as ever. Paloney said, "What did you make of them?"

She looked up. "Thugs," she said.

Julian pulled a little unsure face. "The big one seems okay..." He glanced from one to the other. "All right, perhaps both of them aren't. I don't know. But the other one..."

He looked at Postmistress P and frowned. She said, "Go on, tell him what happened."

Julian stuttered his way through the story, being as fair as his nature would allow to all concerned, and Phil Paloney listened in the same way, until Julian puked on Carter, then he laughed out loud. It was a vision! He said, "I wouldn't have liked to be in the car with that smell all the way back to London." All three turned up their noses.

Julian Crabbe said, "It was almost like he had a fit. Simp, the big one, pulled him off me. I don't quite know what happened, it was all too quick. I think he talked him down. He sat him in the corner, he washed quite a bit of the, ah, well, mess off. Then he gave me some money and they left. After that, I went to the church. Pensioners' coffee morning." Deception now unnecessary, Julian turned and put the tins of fruit back on the shelves and asked, innocently, "Why, did they do something?"

Paloney shook his head and, although he didn't care, asked, "What did you do with the money... Simp, was it, gave you?"

He had to stop himself laughing as the little pink blobs on Julian's cheeks flared red and it was all there in his skittering eyes. The money was in Julian's pocket and it was going to stay there.

When Julian had finished hemming and hawing, Paloney said, "It doesn't matter." He had a sudden urge to give the pair the full info, to bring them into the fold, as it were, but the vicar's dodgy eyes held him back. Soon enough would be soon enough. The thing was, between the two of them, they would probably see just about everybody on the island over the next couple of days, so he needed their help. On the way to the door, he said, "Can you start to put the word about—phone people and all that—we need to have another island meeting, everybody."

"About what?" Postmistress P asked.

As he went out the shop door, Paloney looked over his shoulder. "It's about the ferry. There's been some new developments. There's a chance we can save ourselves. It's really important. We need to organize a meeting fairly quickly. Say Saturday night at the church?" Both started to speak but Paloney stopped them—"I'll explain later"—and was gone with a wave. At that moment there weren't any questions he wanted to answer.

Meanwhile, down South London way, about that time, other family issues were being sorted out. Amber was fed up and she made no bones about it. Eighteen. School was done, it was over, and it didn't matter what her father said, she wasn't going back and she wasn't going to university either. Yes, she probably would have got the right results, but what did that mean? It would just get her on the rail track to middle-class heaven, mortgaged out of her mind. It wasn't going to happen.

Her father had found another way and she wanted a different way again, except she didn't have a clue to what that was. Simp had told her a while back that her dad was like an erratic dynamo and sometimes it went a bit too dynamic and needed a shove to set it straight. She'd seen him giving her dad the pills. There wasn't anything she could do. Her father was what he was and it wasn't always nice. She'd seen his rages, not physical but a bit mental, against her mother when she was young, against Simp when there wasn't anybody else, and, recently, against herself, when she'd turned up all chipper on the doorstep.

Now he stood over her, while she pretended to ignore him and read *NME* on the couch. She had tried to talk to him and now she'd stopped. She turned the pages of the music magazine without really seeing anything, knowing she was annoying him and not caring—that was the plan. Without looking at him, she tossed the magazine aside, got to her feet, and walked over to the window. A little desperate, Carter said, "Amber." Amber looked out on the dull Dulwich street. The house was in a nice part of South London, away from Peckham, away from Carter's business, away from trouble.

The way Amber saw it, if her dad didn't want her to run away from school he shouldn't have bought her a motorbike. It was preposterous for him to argue against the facts, and anyway, yes, she was spoiled, but he could hardly blame her for that, could he? Anyway, there had to be an upside to having a wonky dynamo for a dad, but she hadn't bothered to mentioned that. She turned away from the window and exchanged smiles with Simp. He was a sweetie really. How he'd put up with her dad for all the years was something she didn't understand. She turned on the television. Carter turned it off. Amber stood in front of him, arms folded, and sighed deeply and shook her head. As Carter opened his mouth to speak, Amber spun away, left the room, and closed the door behind her. Carter's shoulders drooped. Exasperated, he said to Simp, "What's she like?"

In the hall, Amber listened at the door, a little smile on her face. Get him with silence—he couldn't stand it for long. She knew what her father was, how he made his money. In that way, he'd been fairly honest with her ever since her early teens, and what he didn't tell her, Uncle Simp usually did. Big softy. She knew, for instance, her father had graduated from armed robbery into clubs and drugs. She could also guess at some of the things the two had to do to keep it all moving. Having someone like Carter for a father matured a person. Once, he'd actually sat down and explained exactly what it was he'd given up, because she was his daughter and he loved her so much. He'd told her, "I couldn't go back to prison after you were born, darling, it wouldn't have been right." Talk about no illusions! It was so sweet, her ever-loving dad had actually given up guns and the prospect of a life in jail, just for her. Yeh, no illusions. She also knew her mother had slapped an ultimatum on him. Told him, "You've got a daughter now, you can't go waving shotguns about as a viable occupation." He'd stopped. Moved sideways, as it were. Probably the one and only time he'd listened to her.

At the far end of the hall was a small toilet. Amber went in, locked the door, and sat down on the closed seat top. She didn't want to use the toilet; she just wanted to get away for a little while. It was a trick she'd picked up in boarding school—the only place she could be really alone and think. The room didn't have a window but an electric vent set high in the wall. It whirred and she listened. It was like being in a box.

Her mother had been a catalog model once. Now she was just another well-kept woman, two steps away, at least, from the reality of what her husband did. Vacuous. The word sounded harsh to Amber, even as she thought it, but the truth was her mother whizzed about like a headless chicken, from this to that, making endless lists about everything that she forgot about almost instantly. There didn't seem to be much beyond the surface. Her mother was strange and unreachable, her father was volatile and unpredictable. How they had ever got together still baffled Amber. The fact that they'd separated soon after she had been sent to boarding school didn't bother her; they were better apart than together. And, for her, easier to manage separately.

Not that Amber was hard; she just had her own coping methods. It was the way her life was. She'd spent most of her early years never knowing what would happen next. Going to boarding school at twelve had been a complete relief for her, a haven, an oasis of rules and regulations, and she thrived on it, and when she'd become friends with some of the other girls, she'd realized some of them had stranger relationships with their parents than she did. But now that was over. It was like a skin she'd wanted to shed for the last year or more. Back home now with her father, she wanted something to do, something that would make her some money.

When she left the toilet and arrived back in the living room, Amber made sure she had a big moody head on her. She stood in front of Carter and wagged a finger at him, as though he were the recalcitrant child, and picked up the argument where they had left off: "No! Don't be obtuse. I don't want some money to go and buy clothes. You can't just throw a few quid at me and think I'll go away. I'm your daughter, remember? Help me. I want to make some quick money, enough to do something. Be a bit independent, yeh? Come on, Dad, you're a drug dealer. If I can't make money with you, who can I make money with? Please?"

This basic discussion had been going on now too long. It seemed like forever, and Carter was exasperated but said nothing. She was his daughter, and in some way he was proud of her, but he just couldn't think in what way that was right at that moment. That pride didn't do him any good, though, because Amber was the one person he couldn't slap down, not really. So he tuned out and let her roll on for a bit. She ground him down, wore him out. Sometimes it seemed he'd been arguing with his daughter her whole life. Involuntarily Carter threw up his arms and then stuffed his hands into his pockets and mooched about the room. His head hurt. It was hard to think when she never let him have the last word.

When did it all change? Did this happen to other parents? What had happened to his little girl? Hadn't he given her everything? What was he supposed to do now? What had she grown into? On my life, he didn't know!

Obdurately, Amber said, "What do you expect me to be like? I'm your daughter."

It was a good tactic. She'd used it before. Carter knew he was being got, but it still got him—it was what family did. Link by sentimental bloody link. Control. None of that stuff had ever worked with him, until Amber.

She got at him. She made him feel emotional. He didn't like emotional. Emotional took him places—uncontrollable places. A sudden vision of himself leaping on that stupid fucking twat of a vicar snapped into his brain. He'd sent the suit to the cleaners, but he knew, deep down, he'd never wear it again. That smiling, genuflecting God-loving cunt! Carter took a couple of breaths, realized he was getting overwrought, and tried to right himself, but what with one thing and another—the lost dope, Stickle, his daughter—he just didn't know. Simp was watching and, before Carter started to tremble, tapped him on the shoulder, put a big arm around him, and together they left the room, Simp reaching in his pocket as they did for the bottle of pills.

Two minutes Amber sat there, biting back, looking calm. By five minutes she was bored and irritated. Ear to the door again, she could hear the murmur of their voices but not what they were saying. She dropped back down onto the couch. At eight minutes, and as she began to wonder if she needed pills of her own to calm her anger, Carter returned, Simp behind him. "Look, my darling, I can't have you out there, know what I mean? Can't have you selling." Amber started to argue and Carter cut her off with hand movements. "Darling, darling, wait, listen, I've got something else you can do. It's a bit out of the ordinary but that's you, ain't it?" He called Simp forward. "Give her the lowdown, tell her like you just told me, go on."

22

It was afternoon when John Newman and Si got together over coffee. They talked a bit about the previous night and about what had happened at Julie's that morning, they talked about the cellars under the Sticks' house, about Dick and his dad, and Si said, "What's it all about with Dick's mum? He's started going to London to see her and talking about leaving—I don't know?"

John Newman said, "People change. I mean, believe it or not, Henry and I played down there in those cellars when we were kids, just like you and Dick did. Sure, we were friends for years, before it all went wrong." He put his second finger over his first and wagged his hand. "We were like that."

John laughed at Si's amazed expression. "He was a lot like Dick as a young man, a bit daft, you know?" Si laughed, and his dad said, "Well, in some ways. I don't mean looks. I know it's hard to see it now, but Henry was a right one when he was young. With him back then, it was all rock and roll, drape suits, brothel creepers, the lot. He left, went to London, and eventually came back here with Sylvie, Dick's mother. She was a nice woman and they would have suited each other well, in another place. She tried hard but she just wasn't a country girl. She wasn't really fit for Stickle, if you know what I mean. A bit like some of the conchies. I reckon if Henry had wanted to keep her, he should never have come back to the island. When Dick was born, Henry was over the moon, but

I don't think it's always the same for women. I guess these days you'd say she had bad postnatal depression. Either that or she just couldn't stand the isolation."

John Newman pushed himself up from his chair and, stretching, walked about the kitchen a bit. He touched things as he mantled and stood gazing out the window for a few moments. He thought about Julie. He thought about D.C. He blew a bit of air out and took some in and thought about how complicated life was sometimes. He knew he didn't have control, had known that ever since his wife had died. Then, as now, he tried to do the right thing, never knowing what the right thing really was. He thought of D.C. and Julie again. D.C. would come around once he'd calmed down, but he wasn't giving up Julie. He looked over at Si. The boy was grown, and himself? He'd been alone too long and Julie was lovely. He definitely wasn't going to give her up.

"I didn't sleep with Sylvie. She came to me because she didn't have anywhere else to go. She arrived here one night with a couple of suitcases. She'd walked over from their farm, wanted to stay and to get the morning ferry to the mainland. She was in bits. You can imagine. A mother doesn't usually leave her child, but I think she'd just had enough. Henry's temper, the isolation, the new baby. I think she was close to a breakdown. Anyway, I let her stay and she left on the morning ferry."

Si watched his dad. It wasn't often he said so much.

John continued: "Henry thought I'd slept with her but I didn't, she just stayed the night. He blamed me, but what was I supposed to do, send her back? We had a bit of a barney."

Si sat back, surprised. "What, like physical?" His dad didn't fight. His dad was Mr. Sensible. John nodded. Si started to laugh and said, "Who won?"

John moved about the kitchen a bit more and, although he didn't answer, slid a sideways smile at his son. He'd beaten Henry but it was pathetic, he didn't want to talk about it, didn't want to explain. Two grown men living a stone's throw from each other, onetime friends who now rarely spoke. Years and years, but some things go deep.

It was late afternoon by the time Petal got to see D.C. They sat across the table from each other in his trailer. D.C. had Petal's hands in his own. The business of Petal's ideas had been dealt with: what she wanted and how she could approach and convince the non-drug-taking community of the plan; how to turn six bales of the best Colombian grass from just a scam into a financial reality. They'd talked about co-ops and bank accounts and how to use the island's smuggling history to help bring the residents together, but that was all just a form of logistics. They also talked about the danger of dealing with Carter and his cronies. The idea of anyone getting hurt didn't sit well with Petal, Julie, or John Newman, and D.C. guessed not with Si or Dipstick either. D.C. knew the threat was for real and didn't bother to deny it. Simp coming up sideways when his back was to the trailer—that had been real enough. He told her. He also told her, "Sometimes you have to kick against the pricks just to remember what it's like to be alive, and when they come, they'll come with a team of Simps, but we've got a whole island." Both admitted it could all get scary, but that wasn't why Petal and D.C. were holding hands.

They were holding hands because D.C. had said, "When your mother wanted to leave London and come down here, I could have stayed in the Smoke. Our marriage was all but over." He shrugged. "I know you know I didn't have a family—foster homes and bloody orphanages was what I had. Well, anyway, I didn't want things to be the same for you, I wanted you to know I was your father. I didn't want history to repeat itself." He shook his head. "I know what I'm like and I know I was lucky to even get to sleep with your mother, let alone have someone like you come from it. Anyway, that's why I came down here to this poxy little island, to be near you. I know I'm not the perfect father but I am here."

Reaching over, Petal took one of his hands in hers and softly touched the fingers. "Dad, Dad, it's—"

But before she could tell him it was all right, D.C. put his other hand over hers and said, "Just let me—look, what I'm asking is please don't reject me, don't cut me out—you're my daughter, I love you. Don't hurt me, please."

For a few moments Petal was dumbstruck. Hurt him. Somehow it had never occurred to her that she, or anyone for that matter, could really hurt her father. Now, all of a sudden, she didn't have a fallback response. She squinted at him. Perhaps he was being honest. As this was D.C., though, she waited for the other shoe to drop. With him, there was always something else, maybe. She waited. Nothing happened. He just squinted back at her. She didn't know what to say or how to act. She couldn't be certain, but it seemed as though he was begging.

Petal didn't know what a begging parent needed. Or what to do with a begging parent. Was there a self-help book? She promised herself to look in a bookshop. Sometime. In the meantime, she looked around the trailer. It was all clean and tidy. He wasn't begging domestic favors. Petal sniffed.

After a silence and a couple of quizzical looks, D.C. said, "Your mother and me, we don't always see eye to eye, but at least we had something. We were in love and"—he cocked his head and looked straight at Petal—"Julie and me, we still love, sometimes."

Petal could have laughed. Like this was news. But she didn't; she'd seen plenty of their parting and plenty of their coming together. If that was love, she wasn't so sure about it.

D.C. shrugged. "Love don't last forever unless you are very lucky. You can love people for all sorts of reasons but that ain't love, do you get me?"

Petal nodded and quietly asked, "What do you think of Dick, Dad? I mean really, you know, and all this moving to London stuff?"

It would have been easy for D.C. to be snide, to laugh and tell her, "If Dipstick could get a GCSE in wanking he'd be proud of it." Trouble was that wasn't even true. Despite the way he looked, he was an all right lad. But nevertheless, the dad-type emotions flickered, faulty and unsure, so D.C. thought carefully and said, "He's all right. His dad's a dick but Dick's okay. Don't like his hair. But you and him? I don't know and can't say, because I don't really know, yeh? But you can tell me if you like."

Petal shirked. Like she'd talk to her father about the boy she was sleeping with. Eh, no way! She still remembered him trying to talk to her about her period. That was bad enough, and anyway, that wasn't what Petal was asking. She didn't need to be told if Dick was good or bad—she was quite capable of deciding that for herself. It was something more intangible.

She'd been going with Dick for nearly a year and she'd always thought they were on the same wavelength. Sometimes she'd even imagined she was in love with him. Now she didn't know. Was she in love? Had she ever been in love? What was love? Sometimes recently she'd looked at Dick and felt next to nothing. Plus, whenever she tried to think straight about Dick, Si's face always seemed to float into her mind. That made it hard to concentrate.

She sighed, blew air, and said, "Like you reckon Mom and you were in love, but how did you know? How did Mum know? Is it like instant?"

D.C. scratched his chin. "Well, it varies I guess, depends. With Julie, for me anyway, it was pretty quick. I was mad about her from the get-go. For me it was like, how lucky do you get? She was good-looking, clever, funny, and best of all, she seemed to like me."

Quiet for a moment, he looked out through the window. Beyond, a half dozen big black crows strutted about on the rough grass of the field like bouncers on crowd control. In the silence, Petal could hear her father's foot as it tapped spasmodically on the trailer floor. A couple of sparrows fluttered down from the blackthorns and were chased away by the crows.

Abruptly, D.C. came forward and rested his elbows on the table. "Still, everything else aside . . ."

Petal froze. She expected him to start pointing his finger at her and telling her something she didn't want to know, but he didn't. Instead, he rested his head in his hands and smiled.

"...there has to be a spark, something basic you can come together about, know what I mean?"

Relieved, Petal said, brightly, "Like music and books, stuff like that?"

D.C. chuckled. "No, yes, of course, but I'm talking much more basic than that. Sex. Look, if you don't get on in bed together, it ain't going to last. Wavelengths ain't the same as orgasms."

Petal froze again. D.C. didn't seem to have the same boundaries as most people, especially other parents. The last time they'd had a conversation as open as this, she'd rushed out of the trailer, her face like a pomegranate, and hadn't come back for months. These days they didn't even try to have any conversations about women's stuff, ever, anymore. End of.

She pulled her mouth down and wrinkled her nose. Behind her the trailer door was propped open, the flight path clear for takeoff. But she'd asked him, and with D.C., mostly you got an answer, like it or not.

D.C. laughed, reached out across the table, and touched her shoulder. "Is that what you want to know? Is that what you're asking me? Because if it is, I'd go further. I'd say it's all in the kiss. If you don't enjoy kissing someone, how long are you going to want to be intimate with them? Imagine going to bed and having sex with someone you don't like kissing for ten, twenty, thirty years. There's a reason most prostitutes don't kiss their punters—it's too intimate."

Older now, Petal didn't run out; she switched, talking of things she had to do, which at the moment mostly involved reading up on cooperative rules. No, she didn't want any more tea. There was this person to go and see and this or that person here or there and someone else over on the other side of the island, so thanks and all that for your help, but, all in all, she thought she better get off. Did she have any better idea of what love was? No, absolutely not, but she determined she would kiss Si if an opportunity came along.

A while later, after Petal had gone, John Newman came through the gate to the field, and as he did so, he could hear D.C. talking to the pig as he threw the mixture of pignuts and swill into the trough. "Poor fucker, three-odd months now and your time is up. But just because I kill you doesn't mean I don't love you or I won't think of you when you're dead." The animal grunted, its nose in the trough. D.C. scratched it roughly behind the ears. "Eating you is a sign of my love. Every time I eat a sausage or slice off a bit of bacon, I'll think of you."

John Newman came and stood beside D.C. at the pig pen. D.C. nodded a hello. They both watched the pig for a while.

D.C. said, "You hungry?"

John Newman said, "What you got?"

The flitch of bacon was in an old pillowcase hanging in the wardrobe. D.C. pulled it free, sliced off a few rashers, tied the pillowcase back around the meat and rehung it on the wardrobe rail. D.C. had thought about Newman and his Julie together, and he understood he'd been stupid that morning, but sometimes he didn't know how to act, only how to react. Ranting and raging, blind and uncaring, was all he could do. When it came to Julie, despite what he'd told Petal, that love they'd had for each other was gone, dead, and now they were more like old friends. He wished it was different. He looked over at John, at his healthy rugged face and at his big work-man-like hands, quiet on the table. Even if it hurt, D.C. knew John was a good man.

They caught each other's eye. Newman sighed and tested D.C. with a crooked little half smile. "I can't help it about Julie. We like each other a lot, D.C., I mean a lot."

D.C. took a loaf he'd made the previous day from the bread bin, cut four slices and laid them on a couple of plates. Over his shoulder, he asked, "Want sauce?" He flipped the rashers and added, "I know, and I've spoken to Petal, and well, I've had time to think."

Newman nodded. "So everything's okay? Yep, sauce on mine. Between us?"

The home-cured bacon smelled good as it spat and sizzled in the pan, and D.C. nodded.

"Got any glasses there?" asked his old friend. From the battered canvas duffel bag at his feet, he took a quart bottle of local cider and poured it into the offered glasses. It was still cold. They clinked them together, swallowed half a glass in a mouthful, and Newman topped them up. D.C. made sand-wiches and sat at the table.

They tucked in, and after a couple of bites, Newman said, quietly, "You know, D.C., you don't have any good reason to be unkind to me. Calling me a taker, that wasn't nice. I know you were hurting over Julie, but it was a bit unnecessary."

D.C. drank the cider in two big gulps, banged the empty glass down, and smiled insincerely. "Me unnecessary! Julie's one thing but you called me a hippie! I ain't and never was a bloody hippie."

They looked straight at each other and began laughing. Newman said, "Bloody hell, D.C., you've been called worse than that!"

D.C. reached over, took up the quart bottle, and poured out two more glasses. "That's not the point. People see you with long hair and put you in a box. Long hair is a fashion statement, not a philosophy, and like I said earlier, that hippie shit is a weak philosophy, it takes you nowhere. Look around the world! We patently ain't all in it together. Anyway, if I'm anything, I'm a bohemian."

Newman started laughing again. "Yeh, we had a few of them here on the farm during the war, when I was a kid. Fancied themselves as artists. Useless when it came to working."

D.C. reached up to the shelf above Newman's head and took down a volume. It was an old dictionary from the 1930s. He opened it and ran through the pages until he found what he wanted. "Here, *bohemian*, 'a person, artist, or writer who lives an unconventional life; a gypsy or one who lives by their wits.'" He pointed a finger at Newman. "I don't think being an artist or writer is mandatory. Personally, I like the last bit best—'one who lives by their wits.'" He held up his glass to Newman. "'One who lives by their wits'—you wouldn't begrudge me that much at least."

Newman laughed, bowed his head in mock surrender, and clinked his glass against D.C.'s. "I'll never call you a hippie again."

23

Sometimes things happen in clusters, so meanwhile after meanwhile, as the day went on, people met, things were arranged, some people sorted out a problem or two, and the vicar and the postmistress punted words around the parish, and in the casual, ad hoc way of Stickle folk, the idea of saving the ferry motivated most, young and old, and a meeting was arranged for the coming Saturday evening, and Paloney did his bit, visited here and there, and others did what they always did, lay on their couch listening to music or the radio, a big fat number hanging from their mouth, and time and tide moved on as it always did, and meanwhile, on the afternoon ferry, a girl on a motorcycle arrived. Amber.

Perhaps Dick could have missed Amber in a crowd, but when he came out of the post office, Stickle Island wasn't crowded, and as Amber took off her helmet and shook her hair free, she saw Dick and smiled. A smile is just a smile. It does not portend a future. It speaks only of the moment, but moments add up. Amber needed somewhere to camp and needed to meet the locals, but at that moment she'd smiled because Dick was a nice-looking guy.

To Dick, when she smiled, it was better than Technicolor and he almost fucking died. He stared stupid, gobsmacked, while his brain tried to catch up and reason. To gain time, he swung his own crash helmet back and forth in his hand as though to say, *Hey, smiling motorcycle riders rule, okay!* He knew it wasn't enough—the swinging thing couldn't last, and then what? He wasn't the greatest of talkers. He looked at the sky and thought about talking about the weather but that was just too pathetic. He thought about motorbikes. Common interest and all that. He pointed to bits on Amber's bike and then they chatted on the way bikers do—and bikers can go on—and they chatted on and made unconscious little body movements: eyes opened wide, tips of tongues flicked, they blinked in unison, they inclined toward each other, and hands were palm up or passive in and out of pockets. And they didn't stop looking at each other. He said things, she said things, and they started to enjoy it, so they said more stuff, they laughed. After a while it was all relax-ay-voo, and by the end Dick was about as happy as he could be and Amber was feeling pretty chipper too. For the time being, whatever mission her father had sent her on was almost forgotten.

Camping? "No problemo!" Of course he knew somewhere to camp.

She laughed. "Speak Spanish then, do you?"

The smile moment had magnified into minutes, and Dick wasn't going to let that slide, so he stuck with another smile. "No, *mon amie*, but I do know somewhere to camp."

They watched each other as they put on their helmets and they watched each other as they cranked up their bikes, and then Dick took her slowly through the farm and out to the field that overlooked Fishtail Bay. It was a beautiful spot: the wide-open sea and the pale blue late-afternoon sky, the crescent beach below, the rich green of the pasture, with the sheep and the gorse bushes dotted here and there. Dick thought briefly of Petal, but he reasoned, *I've not done anything, I'm not doing anything, I'm just standing here.*

Amber had most of what she needed already: a tent, a sleeping bag, a little blue two-burner gas stove with foldaway legs, a couple of small saucepans, two enameled tin mugs, a frying pan, some tinned soup and beans—that kind of thing and, like any sensible girl, a rubber flashlight big enough to concuss any would-be Lotharios.

She told Dick she'd camped many times, and no, the sheep didn't worry her. Dick watched her for two minutes and knew she'd never seen a tent before, and she was looking at the few sheep like they were a pack of wolves. Dick thought, *No one comes here. Why's she here?* Two seconds later she smiled, and a natural-born innocent, he forgot whatever it was he was thinking about.

They erected the tent together, all smiles and silliness and little jokes. Their color was up, their mouths were dry. They avoided touching—bodies were suddenly strange, off-kilter. As he watched her unpack and roll the sleeping bag out inside the tent, Dick tried to comprehend what the fuck was going on. It was like he'd gone into the post office for some stamps and come out and like the whole world had changed, he'd changed. He didn't know if that was possible from one look and a smile, but the world was colored Amber now. He didn't know what had happened or what to do next, but Petal had become once removed. Not in a cruel way, but like she'd become almost historical, anthropological. Something to remember. The past. It wasn't that Amber was better looking or had a better figure than Petal, it wasn't anything like that. It was something else. Something alive was between them, connecting them, and they hadn't even touched.

Dick pointed. "See that stand of trees? That's our house, just behind. I've got like a granny flat at the back. Well, it ain't actually a granny flat, my dad had it built for my grandad." A couple of little jiggy movements and a half laugh gave Dick's soft heart away. His grandad was a man more cantankerous than his own father, but still, he missed him, missed sitting with him as a little chavvy, listening to him curse and remember the first war. Dick shrugged. "Don't worry, he's been dead for years. Anyway, you can come and use the toilet and shower there any time you like, door's never locked." He smiled. "We don't really bother with locking doors much on Stickle."

Amber looked to the trees—it was about seventy yards—she could manage that even if she was desperate. The thought of her dad slid through her mind. "What about thieves?"

Again, Dick shrugged. "Everybody kind of knows each other here. I'll go and get you some water."

At the house Dick found his father crashed out on the couch, where he usually was about that time of day, enjoying a snoozette. Henry's jacket was hung on the back of the door and Dick took the keys to the Land Rover from a pocket. Had his dad been awake, Dick would have asked, but often, the less Henry knew the better. Snooze on.

Dick threw several sacks of logs, a box of fire lighters, milk and tea, bread, sausages, and two full five-gallon plastic containers of water into the vehicle. While he loaded up, he thought about Petal again—how could he not? They had been together about a year, and a year was a long time, and away from Amber now, a little bit of guilt made the blood rise in his face. He wondered what he was doing and what would happen if Petal found out—she had a temper. He also knew he wasn't going to stop. He wanted to be near Amber, regardless of Petal. For the first time in a long time, he didn't know what was going to happen next. It excited and worried him. He waited for something out there in the universe to alter his trajectory, to say, *Look, this is wrong,* but nothing happened. He peered all around at his home, the farm, the sky and trees and everything that made up his world and his understanding of it, and they were all Amber. The sense of guilt left him. He climbed into the Land Rover and started the engine.

Anyway, Dick knew it wasn't all down to him. Ever since he'd talked to her about moving to London, it was like Petal's attitude had cooled. He could feel it, feel the difference even if he didn't really know exactly what the difference was. He knew she didn't want to leave the island; it was one of those things between them. She said this, he said that. Nothing got resolved. And it wasn't just about London. Even though Petal tried to hide it, he could see the way she'd changed toward Si. The looks she gave him. The touches. The way she'd gone off with him in the tractor when they took the dope off the beach. He couldn't figure it out, and now, he wasn't sure he cared.

Back at the tent Dick built a fire. It wasn't cold, they didn't need it, but somehow camping is always better with a fire. As he pulled it together, he checked Amber again about how she'd ended up on Stickle. Amber told half-truths. She was there on her bike. She'd come across on the ferry. She'd found the island by accident. She'd run away from school. Her dad was angry at her. She looked sad, and for Dick, at that time, it was enough. He wasn't thinking about the big picture. He watched Amber whenever he could, and Amber caught his eye when she could and, all smiles, checked him out. They couldn't help themselves. They liked each other. It was there in the air. They held back, neither wanting to ruin something that had hardly started. Each wondering, *Is it? Shall I?* The very air about them was fraught with a longing neither would know actually existed until the moment it was proven—but moments slide, and suddenly Dick remembered his father and jumped up. "Better get the Land Rover back or my old man will go nuts!"

Amber was surprised. "Really?"

Dick nodded. "You know what parents are like!"

When he was gone, she looked about. There was nobody and nothing. She was going to spend the night in a field with sheep. Were sheep like wild animals? What did they eat? Did they hunt in packs? Oh yes, she knew what fathers were like and she knew they had to be manipulated if possible, and she wondered then about Carter and who was manipulating who and what she was doing in the middle of a field on her own. He must have known there was nothing here. Like nothing. No wonder Simp had got her the tent and stuff. In case of emergency. Something was going on with her dad, more than she'd been told. Then, there always was. What he'd wanted—find the grass and tell me where it is—sounded simple enough. Now, she wasn't so sure.

Simp was right, it was very pretty here, but the countryside really wasn't her thing. She'd read *Cold Comfort Farm* at school the year before, and her idea of the countryside was a little confused. And Dick? He was good-looking but he was a country boy. Did she need a clettering stick? Would he bring her vole skins and call her his little mommet? When Dick arrived back on his bike with a flagon of cider, most of her fears were neutralized. She left the flashlight in the tent.

They rinsed out the enameled mugs and filled them with cider. There was no mention of mommets. They drank. They refilled their mugs. They talked about music and Dick said that punk would never die and Amber told him it was already dead. It was a haircut. Dick talked about the Clash, and Amber explained she wasn't talking about the music, she was talking about fashion and style and what was happening now. From that moment on, Dick didn't just like her, he loved her. She talked his language. New ways of looking, small clubs and bands he'd never heard of—it was a high just talking to her.

When Amber asked about his dad, he stopped himself from getting a moan in and said, "We don't really get on. What about you and your dad? What does he do then?"

From where she was sprawled, Amber reached out, picked up a log and pitched it onto the fire. Sparks flew. Amber shrugged and almost smiled. A bit of her wanted to tell him exactly why she was here but another bit said no. One thing her father had always impressed on her was to never tell anyone more than they needed to know. Casually, she said, "Oh, Daddy? This and that, import-export, you know, that type of thing." Wanting to move on, she asked, "Have you lived here all your life?"

Dick wanted to say no, to tell her he'd traveled halfway around the world, but he knew instinctively that kind of bullshit wouldn't wash, and anyway, he didn't want to lie, he wanted Amber to—well, he didn't quite know what. "Right, yeh, but I been around, London, Manchester, seeing bands and stuff. I'm leaving here anyway. Going to move to London. I got ideas." Dick didn't know how he was going to manage to leave or exactly what his ideas were. In his dreams, he saw himself in a club where it was all happening and it was all his doing. It was a dream.

Amber widened her eyes. She had ideas too. "What are you going to do?"

Dick wasn't used to being asked what he was going to do. Mostly his dad shouted at him, but he usually did what he wanted to do and his dad got over it, eventually, and Petal usually told him what she wanted and what she was going to do, and all he had to do was agree. Other times, with other people, he went with the flow because nothing mattered much. Amber was looking at him over the rim of her mug. Her eyes were black and shiny. There was a thin silver ring on one of the fingers holding the mug. It had a tiny heart on it with a red stone in the center. He wanted to reach out and touch it. Touch her. He didn't, couldn't. His head was filled with ideas, with possibilities. Perhaps she would touch him, perhaps somehow money would come his way.

The bales of grass came into his head. Not everybody wanted the same thing, did they? Although he'd been there on the beach from the start and helped all the way, no one was listening to what Dick wanted. The rest of them would scrape and claw to save the ferry, but he wished there could be something, some little bit, for him. Defying this cold hard fact, he said, "Well, I don't really want to talk about it, but there's a bit of money coming my way, maybe."

Burnished by the light of the slowly sinking sun, Dick looked really good to Amber. She drank cider and said, softly, "From your dad?"

Dick hunched his shoulders and shook his head. "No. I won't get anything from him unless I stay and work the farm, or unless he dies."

Family blackmail. Emotional tethering. Amber understood all about that. It was both her parents' forte. You be good, you do this or that, and we'll give you this. That was why she wanted her own money and to be able to get on with her own life. "Do you believe him?" Dick shrugged, she sniggered and said, wickedly, "Is he likely to die soon?"

The mouthful of cider shot halfway down Dick's throat and back up his nose, and he was spluttering and laughing and coughing all at the same time. When he could, he said, "Have you seen my dad? He ain't about to die any time soon." He shook his head. "He's built like a brick shithouse."

Amber was laughing, thinking of her own father. "Mine isn't a brick shithouse, but his friend is!" They laughed again, not really knowing why. Amber said, "My dad's a bit the same. If I want more than he wants to give me, I have to earn it." It wasn't a lie. She was there on the island earning her money, just not right then.

They were quiet, staring at the fire and drinking cider, and when they weren't looking at the fire, they looked out to sea, and far out, near the horizon, they could see tankers and container ships slowly moving through the busy waters of the Channel. They also looked at the sinking sun and the early-evening sky, and when they weren't doing that, they were casting sly glances at each other. After a bit, Dick said, "I got other things, you know, fingers in pies and all that." He wanted to impress her, couldn't help himself. "Do you smoke? You know, dope?"

Amber gave him a big surprised cat's smile, and Dick reached into his shirt pocket and pulled out a baggie of grass. In her heart Amber hoped it was a bit of home grown or some Jamaican commercial. Even if it was the right stuff, she didn't want to jump to any conclusions, because her dad sold a lot of grass, and although Carter didn't know, all through the last eighteen months she'd been selling the same grass to her public school friends. This bit could have arrived here by chance from anywhere, and anyway, there was something about Dick. She felt... *mm*, and that *mm*, it was in her stomach, her chest. It felt good.

He wasn't like the usual guys she ran into. He wasn't an upper-class oik, buoyed by a trust fund, and he wasn't a young geezer, all Pringled up, or even one of the pathetic blockheads who wanted to get in with her father, like she was a doorway they could strut through. A bit shy but not too shy, Dick seemed lovely to Amber. She liked the way he looked and she liked the way he moved. He needed a good haircut but that was all. In her best voice, she said, "Crumbs, I didn't think there would be anything like that down here."

Happily, Dick said, "You'd be surprised."

There was nothing between them except space. Dick swallowed. Neither moved. Three feet was three thousand miles, a gulf. They looked at each other.

With a quick shuffle, Amber cut the space between them in two and said, "Can I have a look?" Dick passed her the bag and Amber stuck her nose inside and sniffed. She knew it, same as, and said, "Smells nice and fresh. Where does it come from, do you think?"

Dick wasn't stupid, merely besotted. "Don't know really. Colombia, I think." Amber, the world was Amber.

They sat side by side as the evening sky darkened. They smoked. Amber threw a couple more logs on the fire. When the joint was done they sat quiet until Amber reached out and gently touched the back of Dick's hand. It was a cattle prod to the heart. They both felt it. Amber left her fingers there for a few moments, linked by an electric current that pulsed in unison with their beating hearts, *bang, bang, bang,* then Dick took her hand and things happened quickly. Hot kisses. Bits of body touched through pushed-aside clothes. The fumble with belts. Cool grass. Hot ashes. Fire roared in their ears. Buttocks, thighs, chest, breasts, the first rising stars, a snap of moon. All pale. A rogue sheep watching. Laughter.

24

The island was small, and whether they wanted to or what, Petal and Dick usually saw each other at some time most days. They rarely needed to hunt each other out. When evening came without sight or sound of the boy, Petal wondered. Where was he? A day like she'd had! Her mother, her father, John Newman, her father again; cycling halfway around the island helping to get people organized for the meeting Saturday night, which wasn't easy when you couldn't tell anyone the actual truth; and taking in all the co-op shit numbed her brain. She needed to talk at somebody. Good or bad, her father wearied her. Made her want to vent. Made her think, even when she didn't want to think. Where was Dick?

She checked in with Si, but he hadn't seen Dick either. Si wasn't worried, easy come, easy —. It was Postmistress P who told Petal about the girl on a motorcycle. So Petal got on her bike one more time and cycled over to Dick's place. He wasn't there. She did a quick circuit of the polytunnels and the swath of soft fruit enclosures. A few heads were still about, working, but none had set eyes on Dick since early that morning. For a moment or two, she thought about going to ask Henry but reckoned it would just be wasted energy. She looked aimlessly here and there, wondered about fate and if this was a sign and did it matter even if it was. After nightfall, she cycled back to the farmhouse and to Dick's flat. All dark, all empty. No motorbike. No Dick.

Leaving the bike, Petal walked around to the side of the house and down past the stand of trees. In the moonlight, she could make out the curling smoke of a dying fire and the gray-green hump of a tent. There was a side to Petal that tended to expect the worst in some situations and sometimes it was the worst. A horrible knot of pain began to revolve in her stomach as she made her way down the field—the end to a perfect day. As she got closer, she could hear the low murmur of voices. Soft laughter. Happiness. This wasn't what she wanted to find. She could guess what he was doing but couldn't deal with the fact that he could do it to her.

She felt a sudden rage. She wanted to rip the tent to shreds with her bare hands, expose them there in their happiness. Her hands were curled and tense like claws, but her fingernails were bitten down. She wanted to be an animal with talons. Her frustration and anger solidified with the knot in her stomach until she felt nauseated. Acid bile crept up her throat and into her nasal passages. She didn't want to puke, she didn't want to cough, she didn't want to make a noise and be discovered, stupid, outside the tent. Petal held her nose and tried to swallow it down. It was foul! She choked silently and staggered back against the two motorbikes, all neat side by side. The bikes clattered over like dominoes with Petal, like an upturned starfish, on top. There were raised voices, a ruckus in the tent, and a rush for the zipper, but before either managed to extricate themselves, Petal had scrambled back to her feet and was up and off.

From behind a nearby gorse bush, she watched. In a way she couldn't quite explain, she felt robbed. And crouched in the dark, she was annoyed that she hadn't thought to kick the bloody motorbikes over on purpose. It was like her rage had been subverted into an accident, a turn of fate. If she had kicked the damn things over, the effect would have been the same, but she would have felt the power of her own actions. She would have been laughing to herself behind the bush instead of cowering. Part of her wanted to reclaim the power she thought she'd lost by jumping up and waving her arms and shouting, but she couldn't, because that would have been just too stupid. She watched surreptitiously while they righted the bikes and laughed about rogue sheep, and then Dick put a couple of fire lighters into the smoldering ashes and set sticks and logs in a pyramid as the flames grew. She'd seen him do the same thing when they'd camped together. The more she watched the more it hurt. They sat together near the fire wrapped in a sleeping bag. They kissed and cuddled. Who was she? The only thing Petal could conceive of was that she was someone he'd met when he'd gone up to London to visit his long-lost mother. Regardless, Petal hadn't seen this coming. Not with Dick. She'd always thought she'd be the one to eventually dump him. When she couldn't stand watching anymore, Petal crept away.

Unable to face breaking down in front of Julie or spending the night alone in her room wide-awake, staring at the ceiling, Petal headed to the Newmans'. Surprised, and a bit apprehensive, Si welcomed her in and made coffee. Shy, he didn't ask her much of anything, but he loved it when she touched his arm and asked if she could stay the night. All innocent. Nothing strange. Both Dick and Petal had spent the night there in the past, together and alone. Then it was all mates. The trouble was, in an abstract, subtle way, this time was different.

When the coffee was made, they went up to his room. Si's bedroom, if you could call it that, was two large rooms knocked together in the upstairs part of the house. It had its own toilet and bath, a mini-kitchen in an alcove, some couches, a TV, a music center, and, behind a kind of half wall, Si's big bed. His father had a similar kind of space on the ground floor. The huge kitchen was their common ground.

Although he wanted to, Si didn't throw shapes he listened. A little while ago, D.C. had lent him *The Women's Room* and *The Female Eunuch*. All right, he hadn't managed to finish all of *The Female Eunuch*, but both books had forced him to think about stuff that was hard to think about, about how women saw the world. He wanted to be sensitive and not overstep the mark. It was time to practice—it would be good for him.

Si patted her back and made sympathetic noises as she cried. She cursed and ranted and made useless threats. Finally, when Petal had talked herself out, he comforted her as best he could. His arm was around her, her head on his chest. They shared a spliff, they exchanged tentative kisses, and they were very sweet, and Petal thought of what D.C. had said about kissing. It was a small intimacy that had been a long time coming. Later, when it seemed right, they touched each other but not too severely. Emotions were involved here, and Si, unknowingly striving for new manhood, trod carefully. For Si, Petal was where she should be—he had loved her since childhood—and he didn't have to rush into anything.

They lounged on a couch, Si made a fire in the grate, and they listened to music.

Si said, "I've dreamed of this since we were—well, it seems like forever."

Petal gazed at his handsome, guileless face. "You didn't say. Why didn't you say?" For her, coming from a family who seemed to have to say everything, always, Si seemed so quiet and self-contained. She reached out, pulled him toward her, kissed his neck, and whispered, "Ah, Si, we've known each other for years, we went to school together. You should have said, you should have told me."

Embarrassed, he said, "I didn't know how. You and Dick seemed..." He stopped for a few seconds, then continued. "Because I'm quiet, that doesn't make me weak. Because I don't try to grab everything I want doesn't make me a fool. I've always known what I think and feel. In the past, you've accused me of letting people take advantage of me, but if they do, it's because I let them, do you get me? I let them— they aren't taking advantage. But when what I want comes my way, then there's no half measures."

That was probably the most Petal had heard him say in one go, ever. Something deep and comforting was running through her bloodstream and it made her feel strange. The flickering light from the fire seemed to touch his face and hair with a golden haze. He looked beautiful. She bit her lip as tears pricked behind her eyes. Crying again—she didn't think so, but she did anyway—and the tears didn't hurt, they were tears of happiness. They slept spooned together. No sex. Slowly, slowly.

Dick knew he was being stupid. Love, especially the instant kind, can make people do strange things. He didn't know where she came from or why she was there, but the desire to share whatever he had with Amber was overwhelming, and regardless of what he'd agreed to with the others, he couldn't, didn't, want to keep the secret. Wrapped together in the sleeping bag by the resurrected fire, he felt closer to Amber than he'd been to anyone in his life. He said, "I've got something to show you."

When she'd left London, Amber had been focused, money on her mind. If she'd had a plan it was basic: arrive, schmooze a few carrot crunchers, discover where the grass was hidden, tell her dad, disappear back to the city, and collect the cash he'd promised her. How hard could it be? But whatever she'd been expecting, meeting Dick had altered her trajectory. Not that she'd forgotten the reason she was there; it was a dilemma pushed, for the moment, to the back of her mind, but it was there and she knew her dad wouldn't wait forever. "What have you got? What are you going to show me?"

Eyes wide, Dick kissed her and grinned. "You'll see. Like I said, fingers in pies and all that. Come on, let's have a little midnight walk."

The night sky was star strewn, the moon yellow. Although they didn't need it, Amber brought the flashlight along. She turned it on and off as they walked, hand in hand, across the fields. At the Newmans' farm, the yard dogs gave a desultory bark as they recognized Dick, then sidled up tails wagging to sniff at Amber. The barn door wasn't locked, but Dick was careful, quiet, as they slipped inside.

They stood in the cavernous dark and Dick flashed the flashlight over the bales. Amber's heart sank. When he spotted the one with the hole in the plastic, he pointed with the flashlight. "Just put your hand in there." She didn't need to do that. She knew already what the bales represented. When she hesitated, Dick said, "Go on, put your hand in and pull a bit out."

Back at the tent, fire stoked again, Dick explained about the council cutting the ferry and about the way the island was and how the loss of the ferry would kill the place. He didn't bother muddying the water with mention of Petal. Nor did he bother with all the old Stick stuff about how his family went back to fuck knows when. None of that mattered anymore. History is for the dead. What Dick wanted with Amber was a brave new world. After he'd explained about the island and the ferry, he explained about how they planned to sell the dope back to the dealer and save the island.

Love and love collided in Amber. Here was a boy, there was a father. She wanted to go with the boy. She imagined leaving the island with him, bringing him back to London. Then she asked him if he felt isolated on Stickle, and he quoted D.C., who'd said one time, "We ain't that isolated. We ain't St. Kilda, we don't eat puffins."

That got Amber so good. She didn't know St. Kilda from a cream egg, but for some reason, the idea of eating puffins made her laugh, but while she was laughing, she thought of her father and wondered then exactly what she was doing. She thought about the way people talked about family and talked about blood ties, but when it came to family, they didn't talk about right and wrong. She didn't like what she thought, but despite her feelings she still couldn't say, couldn't explain to Dick why she was there. Couldn't talk. Blocked. Unable. Instead she kissed him and kissed him and told herself she would explain later.

After a while, Dick said, "I'm hoping maybe to get some of the money from the dope, so I can go to London and get something going." And, nervously, he continued. "It's just a dream really. I'd—I'd like to get into music but like I'm not musical." He twisted his mouth, hunched his shoulders, smiled. "Don't laugh, but like I'd like to maybe start some sort of a music club, you know?"

Amber didn't laugh. She came forward slightly from where she sat and stared into his eyes. "Really?" This was like more than fate, more than kismet. She kissed him, very seriously, and said, "Now, don't you laugh! That's what I want to do too!"

This minute, this hour, this day, this year, love needs confirmation and the idea of a future, however hazy. Love looks forward, and Dick was already in the future. He opened up. "Look, I know we have only just—" He stopped and ran the palm of his hand gently down her arm, got shy, and then he came back. "But I was thinking about what you said, you know, about new music, new styles. Made me think. Maybe something like that. Maybe if we could get the money, maybe we could do it together?"

It was late when they finally fell asleep, but it was early when Dick left the tent. Amber slept on. It was Friday.

Although he may have just fallen in love, a farm was still a farm, ticktock it didn't stop. But the young man was so loved up, nothing touched him. Everything was one step beyond. Even some of the questions he should have asked. It was a kind of dreamy remote control. He did everything he needed to do, but all he thought about was Amber. Nevertheless, he managed to keep one eye on the coming night and the moving of the bales. Whatever else was on his mind, he was determined Henry would be on the morning ferry.

Father and son ate early bacon sandwiches around the Rayburn and decided on the glass and other things they needed on the mainland. There was a trailer load of soft fruit and other produce to take to the wholesaler, which Dick had made ready and hitched up to the Land Rover. While they ate, Dick explained about the tent in the field. Not exactly of course. Henry hated having anybody unnecessary on his land. When he questioned his son on what she wanted, what she was doing and why she was there, Dick lied. He told his dad she was on a field trip from her school, a project about shipping traffic in the Channel. Henry moaned and grumbled that no one in her right mind came to Stickle, but to no avail. What could he do? Dick had learned years ago that if he wanted to do anything he knew his father would disagree with, it was best to present him with a fait accompli.

He explained, "You were asleep—I didn't think you'd mind. She's a nice girl, no trouble-like. I told her she could use my shower and toilet. So, no problem." He nodded his head as though every word was the God's honest. Henry muttered on about strangers on the land for a bit more, and Dick smiled and shrugged. "Don't worry, Dad, all she's doing is counting ships. Go to Dymchurch, have a good time. No worries. I'll see you Saturday night when you get back."

Later, after Henry had left, Dick supervised the pickers and packers, but by midday, he was back at the tent. Amber fried sausages and eggs. After they had eaten, they went down to the beach and swam. The sea was blue and chill with little whitecaps that slapped them in the face and made them laugh. They had showers at the house and then they spent time playing Dick's records, exchanging little confidences and body fluids.

Henry went off in innocence and did what most people do throughout most of their lives, nothing much. He went to the glaziers and the builders' merchant, the fruit wholesalers, and he went to the café and then the pub. He ran into a few people he knew. They went for food, then to another pub. Nothing untoward—a few laughs with the men and a bit of mild flirtation here and there with women he'd known casually for years. He was relaxed, happy. When asked about Dick, it was easy to say everything was all right, good, the boy was doing well. It struck him, as it had in the past, how merely crossing the narrow stretch of sea between Dymchurch and the island made a difference to his way of thinking and behaving. Again, he thought of change and what it would be like and wondered if he should just give Dick the money he had put aside for him so the lad could leave guilt-free, and they could both get on with new lives. It would be hard, but his mind had begun to turn and it felt good. Later he slept justified in a nice attic room above the pub, near the quay. In the morning, someone would call him and give him a big fried breakfast, and then he would spend the rest of the day drinking around the town, before catching the afternoon ferry back home to Stickle.

25

Everything Dick had done since he'd walked out of the post office the previous afternoon was like a movie run over and over, until all the colors had leached and blended into Amber. It had been an intense, almost sleepless twenty-four hours for both of them. By late Friday afternoon, Amber, who had her own concerns, went back to her tent and lay on her sleeping bag and wondered what she would tell her father. Dick, due to help move the bales after dark, was weary and crashed out on his bed.

Evening came around. A sound roused Dick. The falling of the backdoor latch or the click of the hall light switch, and then, through sleep-washed eyes, he saw Petal hesitate on the bedroom's threshold. She stood in the doorway, a dim halo of creamy luminescence highlighting her pink hair. She still looked good, she was still the same person. That was the trouble. He'd changed.

As she came over to the bed, Petal reached out to touch him, and he recoiled a fraction. It was the very smallest of movements but, for Petal, a moment of truth. It was all she needed. Petal was like her dad: calm, collected, volatile, and sometimes all at once. She half crouched over him. "What's up?"

He felt the chill and tried to smile, to behave normally, but that wasn't going to happen. Even he knew the truth. Petal had him bang to rights.

The truth was it was all she could do to restrain herself from hitting him. Through gritted teeth she said, levelly, "Where have you been? Haven't seen you. Are you all right?"

Somewhere, a bit of her wanted him to try to explain. She wanted to hear him say how he'd made a stupid mistake. Apologize on bended knee or something like that. She wanted to laugh at him while he tried to explain that what she thought was happening wasn't happening, and it was all a big mistake, and he was helping the poor girl find something in the dark and they were lying down because the tent was quite small. She'd let him talk himself up a mountain and then kick him off.

All of a sudden, a splurt, a little cameo of her cuddled in Si's arms, shot into her brain. Snapping straight, she said, "It's over. Keep her away from me. We're meeting at the Newmans' to move the bales."

Outside the shop, in Stickle's lone phone box, Amber talked to Carter. The first mistake she'd made was telling him where the barn was. Carter was pleased and chuntered on, told her it was good work. Amber didn't want to hear, only half listened and wished Dick had never shown her the bales of grass. She wished she didn't know that the barn doors weren't locked, wished she didn't know how easy it would be for Carter to come down and just take everything.

Meeting Dick had changed things. She liked the way he looked, she liked the way he talked, but what had touched Amber's heart was that Dick wanted her enough to put everything at risk like that, in innocence. Amber saw it like the truth of a person opened out for you to see, and Dick had reached her deep down, and she wondered about herself. What kind of person would hurt someone like that? Then she remembered she was supposed to be talking to her father and tuned back in.

She tried to explain about saving the ferry and the other stuff Dick had told her, but Carter was never a bleeding heart. He told her he'd offered ten grand to D.C. and that was that. Nothing more.

Amber said, "Can't we negotiate? These people aren't like you, you don't have to come down heavy, please."

Never. He had a business to run and that was the offer. He didn't care about some bloody little island. If she could get it at that price, she'd get her ten as well. As Carter pointed out, fair's fair.

The second mistake Amber made was trying to reason with him. Because she'd always had everything, because he'd always been generous to her, the way he viewed money was something she didn't understand. For him it was essential. It made him tick. Every pound was personal. He remembered having to rob and steal just to eat. As he'd told her a while ago, "You don't go back there." No, Carter didn't look back, he looked to his money. In this deal, Carter saw only money lost. Cash down the toilet. The Colombians may have written it off as an act of God, but Carter didn't believe in God or any other motherfucker, and even his daughter couldn't reason with him on that.

Even though Amber thought she had her father wrapped around her little finger most of the time, men are just men and sometimes they shout, and even though he loved Amber, that was what Carter did. "I thought you were the one that wanted to make some money! What's up? One way or the other, I'm coming down on Sunday and I'm taking those bales back with me. Tell those fucking carrot crunchers to stay out of my way. I'll have the ten grand with me and some of the boys, so tell them it's pay or play."

Amber closed her eyes, held the phone like a hammer in her hand and tapped it gently against her forehead.

Carter smacked the phone down. What was the matter with these people? They get to a poxy little island and lose half their brain. Simp was still wittering on about the place—how it reminded him of being a chavvy and how he'd like to spend time there, get back to nature and all that fucking shit—and now Amber was on the same tip. Wanted to save the world with his money! No fucking chance!

Night crept over the island. The tent was lonely. The fire was out. Unsure, confused, Amber built another fire. It was a weak, wispy thing, neither of use nor comfort. She sat beside it and poked it with a stick, which didn't help. She waited. Dick had told her there was some job or the other to do, and he'd meet her when he was finished. Her head was full of Dick, in the nicest possible way. Dick and more Dick, and she realized, sometimes the person you thought you were, the person who'd do anything to get what you wanted, didn't actually exist, and somehow your heart had become so full you didn't know what to do with it. It was a 180-degree thing. It took time to adjust. She worried about what her father would do. What the islanders would do. What Dick would do when he found out who her father was. Even though she hardly admitted it to herself, Amber knew she couldn't sell Dick out, but she didn't know how to tell him the truth either.

The sheep were huddled all together in the gloom, their little red-and-white eyes staring. Were they looking at her? When she'd read Stephen King's *Salem's Lot*, she'd made sure her windows were shut at night for months after. The book had ended up with so many vampires, they'd resorted to drinking animal blood. If a vampire drinks sheep's blood, do the sheep become vampires? It was a question the book never really answered.

The dark, the quiet, the wide-open space, the sheep, the crap fire, Dick, her dad—too much was zipping around in her mind. What she needed was a little room with a lock on the door where she could sit with her head in her hands and think.

She walked off toward the house. She wanted to see Dick, to say something, nothing, just to see him and use the toilet. There was engine noise off up the other side somewhere, and she assumed now, in the modern world, farmers were like everybody else and went 24-7. Lettuce doesn't grow itself.

The granddaddy flat was deserted, but she went through into the living room and back to the toilet. It was old school with nothing but the bare necessities: toilet paper, a flush toilet, a bolt on the door. It was painted green and white, and there were pictures of punk performers torn from *Sniffin' Glue* and *NME* stuck to the walls. It could have been a real nice respite—all quiet, locked in a little room, a chance to collect her thoughts—but it wasn't. There was a rumbling down below and it wasn't her stomach. Some of the tractor-type noises she'd heard on her way in now seemed right below her. Backward and forward. What was going on? She pulled herself together and went to have a look.

Around the corner of the house, a light from a spot on the front of the tractor bathed the back of the building in chopped-up chunks of bright glare and deep shadow. The engine rumbled. A bale of grass was on the forks of the tractor. There was a girl and a big guy in the tractor's cab. On the ramp leading down into the cellar, waving the tractor forward, was an older guy with long hair. No sign of Dick. It was easy for Amber to guess what was happening and it was a bit of a relief. Probably wouldn't do Amber any good in the long run, but the idea that her father would hare down to the island on Sunday and find absolutely nothing tickled her at that moment.

D.C. held up his hand to halt the tractor's progress and came to the side door. He pointed to Amber and shouted above the noise, "Who's she?"

Petal opened the cab door. "I know who she is but I don't trust her! She doesn't look like much of a camper, and who camps on Stickle anyway?"

"Her timing is odd," D.C. admitted.

"How do we know she's not one of them, eh?" Petal jumped from the tractor. Si turned off the engine and Petal made straight for Amber. "Looking for him?" She spat out a gob of harsh laughter. "You want him, you can have him, and good luck to you! I hope you get more sense out of him than I ever did." She started to wave her arms. "Now get away, go on, go back to your scabby little tent, you—you bloody grockle!"

Amber stepped forward. Petal didn't scare her. Public school and having Carter for a father had taught her certain things; backing down wasn't one of them. Petal was jabbing a finger as she spoke. Ambers fists were clenched by her side.

Having heard the tractor engine cut out, Dick wandered up from the cellar. He saw Amber and Petal standing nearly nose to nose, bright with big shadows; D.C. looking nonplussed; and Si climbing down from the tractor. New love, ex-girlfriend, ex-girlfriend's dad, girlfriend's best friend and his own best mate: not an ideal situation in which to sort out your love life. Dick shuffled toward the men and tried to explain: "Her name's Amber." He waved vaguely toward the field, avoiding eye contact with anybody. "She's staying in a tent for a few days."

D.C. asked, "Do you think she knows what's going on?"

"No, she's got no idea, why would she?" Dick lied.

D.C. frowned, watching the two women sizing each other up. "What's up with Petal, then? She looks pretty angry."

Dick swallowed uncomfortably. "She—she..." He looked about in a kind of daze.

Suddenly D.C. understood and shook his head. "You been playing away?"

Dick couldn't answer. His head dropped. He knew, D.C. knew, Si knew. Dick shoved his hands deep in the pockets of his jeans and hunched his shoulders. Si and Dick looked at each other and pulled unhappy faces. Even if it were needed, they didn't have a fight in them. The three of them watched the two girls. It was a standoff. Finally, with a hand on Dick's back, D.C. shoved. "You better get over there, lover boy."

It wasn't that far but it felt far. Si said, "Dead man walking." D.C. laughed.

Dick looked back at them. Under his breath, he pleaded, "I don't know what to say or what to do."

D.C. and Si seemed not *not* to hear him, and he found himself walking slowly over. But by then, Petal and Amber had things sussed, though they weren't about to become friends. Love is more basic, feral, animal, and even before Dick reached them, Amber took a chance and nodded toward the tractor, where Si stood. "That's your bloke over there, isn't it?"

Was it that obvious? Petal couldn't help a quick glance over her shoulder, and Amber looked toward Dick. The girls knew what was what, and by the time Dick had dragged his sorry arse over to them, all was quiet. The two girls were standing tense, shoulders squared, lips curled. But it was all shake and bake. They knew the truth.

Petal said, "Fuck you."

Amber said, "And fuck you too."

Love rules.

Dick finally arrived trying to apologize: "I'm sorry, Petal, I didn't know this could—" He stumbled over the words. Although he felt like it, Dick wasn't the bad man, the backstairs crawler, the man with co-respondents shoes. He was a young guy. Things happened and the blame wasn't all his, at least he didn't think it was, but what the fuck did he know? Petal spat at his feet, and when he tried again, he made it worse. "It's not you, it's me."

Petal took it with two fingers in his face and a big round "Fuck you." She stalked back to the tractor, angry, but not so angry she couldn't see that in the weird black-and-white glare of the spot, Si's blond hair, ruffled by the breeze and just long enough to be annoying, made him look like a minor Greek god. Her bottom lip hung sullenly, her eyes were dark, and for absolutely no reason, she punched Si hard on the arm.

Si said, "What have I done?"

Petal said, "You haven't done anything."

Back at the tent, Amber flopped down on the grass and held her head in her hands. She wasn't a crier, but tears stung her eyes. Her dad was probably right after all—trust no one. "That's your girlfriend then, is it?"

Dick started to make a fire. Quietly, he said, "Ex." A few minutes and it was roaring.

Amber said, sadly, "How do you do that?"

Dick glanced at her and smiled. "Practice."

Amber didn't return the smile. "Like with me, is that what I am? Practice?" Dick fiddled with the fire. With a cold tilt to her voice, Amber said, "So I'm a grockle, am I? Do many grockles come here? Many girls like me? Is that what you do? No wonder she was angry."

Dick knew that was ridiculous—tourists rarely came to Stickle, and a girl like Amber, never. He blurted out, "I've only been with one girl before you and that was Petal."

Amber didn't altogether believe his reply, and she curled her lip. "She's with that other guy, right?"

Dick shrugged, sighed, rolled his head in a yes-no fashion, and admitted, grudgingly, "Suppose she is now." It was more than difficult to explain—how it had already almost been over anyway and that Petal had already begun to tire of him. Nobody in his right mind would tell a new love something like that.

"For such a little place, you people like to put yourselves about, don't you?"

He reached out for Amber's hand, but she swatted him away.

"Don't."

They didn't speak. They stared at the fire. Time went by. What Dick wanted at that moment was all the language, all the words, everything he'd never bothered to learn about the beauty of English, and he wanted to be able to roll and flow, to tell Amber in a concise, articulated string of words exactly about this and that and everything, but his brain was numb with thinking, and Petal and Amber were like two different worlds that should never collide but they had, and there weren't sentences he could think of to explain that. So Dick put some wood on the fire and again tried to reach for Amber's hand. It was cool and dry, and their fingers entwined. They both breathed out then, as though they'd been holding their breath for hours, days, lifetimes. Neither spoke. The touch was enough.

Their bodies moved inexorably closer, inch by slow inch. Dick shifted away from the fire to look into her eyes. They weren't arguing. They were adjusting.

She stuttered, "I-I-I—"

He said, "I know, I know. I'm sorry." He paused. "I swear, honestly, I haven't. No one comes here and I haven't and I've never felt like this before." He shook his head and said hurriedly, "I think I love you. Does that sound stupid?"

That was exactly what Amber wanted to hear. She kissed him and, more, she said, "Me too."

They dillydallied the way folks do, they touched each other up. It wasn't over, it was touch and feel about, hands up legs and fingers curled about an ankle, hands slipping between thighs, nipples that needed kissing. They slipped in and they slipped out, they moved about and went on little runs of quick movements, and every touch was for real. Neither questioned the moment or the fucking past or the fucking future.

Later, Dick told her, "So we all agreed not to tell anybody. Then I showed you. All right, I love you, but it was a bit stupid. Anyway, I didn't tell you we were moving the stuff because I felt bad for the others, like I'd let them down. I'm sorry. This is all new to me, everything is new to me. Honest, look, when this is done, money or not, I'm moving to London."

Now was the moment for Amber to come out with it, now was the moment of truth: the time to tell him about herself and the reason she was there. And she wanted to tell him. She was determined to tell him. She needed to tell him. But still, there was her dad. There was Carter. A problem she could not solve, impossible to talk about. She tilted her head a little bit so Dick could kiss her. It had been a long day. She would tell him in the morning.

26

It was Saturday evening on Stickle. There wasn't anywhere else to go. Nothing else was happening. They came along in dribs and drabs and stood around under the lee of the church and wondered what it was all about. The old-timers and the blow-ins. They milled about swapping information that was basically the same. They all believed it was about the ferry. They murmured about possible changes to the council's policy, wondered if the bastard councillor would ever show his face again. There were jokes about tar and feathers or throwing him into the bay. The fact that Tony and Dave, the father-and-son team who ran the ferry, were there, talking to D.C., seemed to confirm it.

Chatting as they went, they filed in and sat in pews. Making his way toward a seat, John Newman scanned the church. The only noticeable absence was Henry Stick. John said to Dick, "I thought you said your dad would be here tonight."

Dick shrugged. He'd left a note telling him about the meeting but honestly didn't know if he wanted his father there or not, didn't want to explain about the dope in the cellar that, he was almost 100 percent positive, Henry wouldn't agree with anyway. The best thing would be if the whole deal was done and dusted before his father arrived.

Julian Crabbe clapped his hands and, after about half a minute, managed to call the meeting to order. There were shouts from the floor: "Why are we here?" "What are we here for?" "What about the ferry?" "I thought we'd got till next April."

The vicar looked at Paloney and Petal, who looked at each other. Under his breath, Paloney said, "You're on."

At that moment, with the church full of people, Petal felt suddenly weak, almost nauseated and glued to the pew. Finally, actually physically prodded by Paloney and D.C., she rose on shaky legs. She looked about at all the people and took a deep breath. "Whatever our differences, we all want to live here on the island, so why don't we join together and try to make it our island?" What was she saying? Even to herself she sounded like an idiot.

A man at the back laughed and shouted, "How are we going to do that?" D.C. had a hand over his mouth, and his shoulders shook with laughter. Julie looked perplexed. John Newman's lips were pursed.

Annoyed with herself, Petal tried again. "Look, after the storms something was washed up on the beach. It's valuable."

Voices came back to her in a clutch: "What?" "Washed up?" "What is it?" "What's been found?" "How much is it worth?"

Petal tried to think of a way to soft-soap the situation and looked again over to Julie and D.C., who sat with John Newman on the pews a couple of rows back. D.C., more hindrance than help, grinned and shrugged. He was beginning to annoy Petal, and in a way, it helped her. Sod him. Julie mouthed, "Go on."

Petal looked out on the full church, and for a moment she caught Si's eye. He was giving her a look, all half closed like Elvis or somebody. His lips were pink and moist. He looked beautiful. She wanted his love. Strength began to come back to her legs. This was something she had to do. She'd studied up on co-ops, and although she didn't completely understand it all, she now knew enough to get the ball rolling. Petal held up her hands. "Okay, okay, this is the tricky bit."

She paused. "What we've found is illegal, but it could save the ferry and the island." The moment of truth. "It's six bales of Colombian grass, and it's worth a lot of money."

Silence, a big long silence. Eventually the question was asked several times all at once. Simply, "How much?"

"Two million, but we'd be seeking a share of two hundred thousand," Petal said. "And with two hundred thousand, we could run the ferry ourselves as a co-op."

A hippie with dreads stood up and spoke in a bored monotone: "Most things are about money, man. Why does everything have to be about money? The world's a beautiful place, why do we have to spoil it with greed?"

Some people coughed, others laughed, and a few heavy sighs blew about the room. Petal smiled at the stoned individual. This she could deal with. "All right, okay, but this money would be shared between us. We would all own the ferry. It's about our island and being able to maintain our life here."

"It's still about money," the dreaded hippie muttered.

"What ideas do you have to save the island?" Petal's smile had not left her face.

Nonplussed, he eyed the congregation uncertainly. "Ideas? I don't know, man, I was just saying, you know, like why?"

More people laughed and Petal said, swiftly, "Yes, right, thanks for that. Now anybody else with any useful ideas?"

Plenty of people had questions, and between Petal and PC Paloney, most were answered, but for some, the amount of money mentioned was almost too much, like Monopoly money. Most had no real concept of what was involved. Could they go to jail if it went wrong? Who would buy it? It was hard to grasp.

D.C. tried in his own way to help, waving an arm toward Julian Crabbe. "If you believe in God, this is God given; if you believe in luck, this is pure, the very best of luck. If you believe in fate, this is what fate looks like. When the council arbitrarily takes away our democratic rights to live where and how we choose, it's time to stand up and be counted. This isn't about us all making a few quid. This is about seeing the way things are and keeping your way of life. This could be our one chance to take back control and, if you like, stick two fingers up at the powers that be."

There were shouts of agreement. Paloney waved D.C. back into his seat.

Petal, pulling out her notes on cooperative planning, began to explain that the money would be held in common. "It's a bit like what those old-time lefties used to go on about, you know, taking control of the means of production." Petal had no real idea exactly what that meant, but she'd heard her dad say it and liked the sound of it.

Someone else near the back shouted, "Hasn't seemed to have done those poor fucking collective farmers in Russia much good."

Someone with half a brain asked, "So are you saying we sell the dope and buy and run the ferry?"

"Yes, that's more or less it," Petal said. "There are rules and regulations to starting a co-op, so it will take a little bit of effort and luck, but yes, the plan would be to form a co-op and use the drug money to fund it. Everyone on the island would be a member, so the money would appear to come from us all, which would explain the large amount. Then we run the ferry as a non-profit-making venture."

Someone else sensible asked, "What about the guys who own the ferry? Why would they agree to that? It's their livelihood."

"Well, then they can join the co-op and we'll give them jobs," Julie interjected, hopefully.

D.C. couldn't help but sneer. "Well, they're going to lose it anyway if Kent Cunty Council have their way."

Some people sniggered. Enough was enough, and Petal snapped, "Why don't you shut up. This isn't a joke, Dad."

Another fella pushed himself to his feet. "All right then, but how do you know Dave and Tony would want to—"

Tony waved from the back of the church. "We're here, Bert, ain't we?"

Bert swiveled and waved back. "Sorry, lads, didn't see you there."

Tony looked at his son, who shrugged and said, "From our point of view, if we don't agree, it's all over anyway come April. Really, we haven't got a lot to lose."

John Newman asked, "How much do you think the actual ferry is worth?"

Tony shook his head. "Well, after next April it won't be worth a lot, will it?" He shrugged and thought for a minute or two. "It's hard to say, but if we had to sell it, we'd get maybe twenty thousand. That's if we could sell it."

There was a bit of a silence while people thought about it. Then, as though the idea had finally sunk in, several islanders stood to have their say.

Des, a guy of about thirty with a smeggy beard, went first. "My family have been on this island for nearly three hundred years. And from what I've been told, it seems this place always needed something nefarious to survive. What does it matter, tastes change. Way back it was French lace and brandy. Now it's this stuff."

Next was Bill. He was small and bulky. His wife and two teen-type chavvies were next to him. "All that stuff you read in the papers about drugs is rubbish. It's like drink, it depends on you. I tried that hashish and opium when I was in India with the army, just after the war. I'm still here. Anyway, as D.C. said, it's like the bounty of the sea. I'm for it."

An old woman, Maude, in a long cardigan, raised her walking stick. "I don't know about that, but what will hap-

pen to us if we don't? I've had a good think since that councillor was here. What will they do with us, eh? We'll be like
those poor refugees, those Vietnamese boat people. Pushed
from pillar to post. I'm too old to be shifting."

A score of other crumblies all started shouting together.
They weren't going to move. They'd faced down Hitler when
he was just across the Channel, and they weren't going to let
some jumped-up local official tell them where they could live.
When they'd coughed themselves into silence and collapsed
back into their seats, Liz, a woman in her thirties with drab
blond hair and a couple of kids beside her, raised a hand.
"Isn't there another way? You know, couldn't we complain?
Couldn't we get the council's decision reversed?"

Everybody sat there looking at one another for a while.
Some there may have claimed everything is political, but
modern politics wasn't about change or progress, it was all
about maintaining the status quo for big business and the
multinationals. While on the surface of it, the idea may have
sounded reasonable, if there was one thing nearly all the Islanders agreed on, it was that politics wasn't going to solve
any of their problems. And hardly a person in that church,
including Julian Crabbe, believed in miracles.

But Postmistress P interrupted Petal before she could
respond. Even before Paloney had asked her to help organize this meeting, she'd put some of the pieces together, the
two from London and them wanting to find D.C. Something
to do with drugs. If it meant that the island could survive,
she was for it. On her feet, Penelope sucked her teeth. "Liz,
Thatcher isn't a politician, you can't expect a change of policy from her; she's a thug, a juggernaut, she just rolls over you."

Maybe it was her tone of voice or some element of threat
in P's posture, but the other woman drew her children toward her and said, defiantly, "I voted for Maggie."

Sweetly, the postmistress replied, "I hope she has made you very happy."

With the shop and post office, most things passed through Penelope's hands or were heard by her ears or seen by her eyes. Had she wanted to, she could say plenty about the finances of the island, the black economy, the work on the farms and the effects on the island of the blow-ins. Penelope knew because she cashed their dole checks, dished out the old age peeps' pensions, gave credit late in the week. As D.C. said, it was time to stand up.

She said, "We all have our own ideas about what is right or wrong, but I agree with Petal, this is an opportunity, we should come together, and a co-op is a really good idea. Come on, let's show a bit of community spirit. This is like a gift, and if we can keep the island going with this money, I, for one, think we should." She paused and there was a nodding of heads and glances of agreement. She wasn't finished. "On another note, I know some of you here don't like the blow-ins, but they have brought new life to the island. The place was on its last legs ten years ago. There were barely enough people to work the farms, and regardless of what some of you think, without the blow-ins the island would already be dead. They keep the post office and the shop open."

Ethel, a tough-looking old bird of about sixty in a man's flat cap, chipped in. "I moved here in the fifties. I was a blow-in back then, but I'm still here. This is my home and I'm not moving even if they cut the ferry. I agree with the postmistress. If this is the only way, I'm for it."

The hippie nervously raised his hand again. "Can't we keep some?"

Quite a few of the blow-ins laughed. D.C. swung around in his seat. "Well, most of us that like a puff have already had some and you too, but this ain't about ten quids' worth of grass. This is about everybody on the island. This is about our survival."

He pulled a spliff out of his top pocket, sparked it up, and took a long pull. As he exhaled he held the joint out for any takers—no one moved, not even the hippie, who was too far back. D.C. took another pull and the sweet, pungent odor drifted in eddies among the villagers. Nostrils flared but still there were no takers. D.C. took another drag and held it up again.

Paloney took the joint and held it aloft, the disbelieving stares of the islanders upon him. "I know I'm supposed to uphold the law, but I became a policeman to serve people and I'm here to serve this island. Maybe I wasn't born here, but I want the best for this island, and in that way, I am one of you. I know I've only been here a comparative short while, but I feel it's my home too. I don't want to have to leave—I say let's take the bounty of the sea."

And then, ceremoniously, he handed the joint back to D.C., un-toked.

27

When Henry Stick arrived back at the house all was quiet. Dick didn't seem to be around. He went to his favored spot, the long couch in the living room, and lay down to sleep off the few beers he'd had that afternoon. When he awoke he had a shower and went to the kitchen to make a sandwich and saw Dick's note about the meeting, propped on the table. Dick had omitted to give a time when the meeting started or what it was about. Henry went to Dick's flat to see if the lad had already left.

Meanwhile, half an hour earlier, Amber had made a big decision. Her father, and what she'd told him and what he could do, sat heavy on her. She knew it was emotional, knew that if she hadn't run into Dick, she probably wouldn't care. But everything had changed. Doing the dirty on your own father didn't feel right, but there wasn't any other option. Love had her. Amber had to tell Dick the truth, it had become an imperative. If she didn't it would be a blight on every moment they had enjoyed and a blight on any future they may have.

When she arrived at Dick's flat he wasn't there. She flopped onto the couch, not sure now what to do. He'd already gone to the church for the meeting, and for a moment she thought about going to tell him, but the idea was just too scary. Amber could muster enough nerve to tell Dick about her dad, but not the whole island. She jumped to her feet when she heard the outside door opening and ran into the hall. "Dick, we've got to talk! I've got something I have to tell you, something I really, really should have told you already. It's important. It's about—"

Henry, whiskers and hair slicked back like some kind of shambling hillbilly, was a surprise. She stopped in her tracks. It wasn't hard to guess that the man before her was Dick's father. He was big, like a version of Simp gone to seed, but there was enough of his son there, in the eyes and the shoulders. Amber tried to stay calm, but there was already too much, just too much. This wasn't the moment to meet the new boyfriend's father.

Amber didn't often cry, didn't want to cry, but control was slipping and she could feel the tears damming up behind her eyes. The only thing Dick had told her about his dad was that he liked to shout. One thing she didn't think she could deal with right now was being shouted at. Her own father shouted, and if she didn't find Dick and warn him, her dad would arrive in the morning and something nasty would happen. This wasn't how things were supposed to be. When people said love altered everything, and it did, was this what they meant? Despite herself, Amber burst into tears. "I haven't done anything! Please don't shout at me, please!"

Henry stopped in his tracks, figuring that this must be the girl from the tent. Shout? He was in a fine mood, why would he want to shout? He'd settled, almost, on a decision. Anyway, he didn't know this girl, and what's more, you couldn't shout at a crying girl. Could you? On the other hand, you couldn't have strangers wandering about your house willy-nilly. He tried not to sound too gruff. "What's so important?" When she didn't answer, he waved vaguely in her direction. "Well?"

Amber sobbed, "I thought you were Dick but he must already be at that meeting."

A little patch of carpet splashed with evening sunlight caught her eye and she looked down at it, and half of her hoped when she looked back up again he would be gone, but he was still there. Haltingly, she said, "They are all at that meeting."

Henry's big loose mouth blew an involuntary sigh of disdain. He hated bloody meetings. "And?"

In over her head with Dick's father, her father, both fathers, the situation, Dick, everything, Amber was at a loss. She prevaricated through her tears. "Don't know, but Dick said the whole island was involved. It's complicated."

Most of the time Henry didn't do complicated, but he made an effort. Something was going on and he needed to catch up. Meetings these days usually had something to do with the ferry. "Okay. If it's about the ferry, I'm a part, a big part, of this island. Why ain't I involved?" Even when Henry didn't mean to sound harsh, he sounded harsh. Amber ducked her head, like a dog waiting for a kick, and Henry tried to tone it down further, way down into something that wouldn't scare a newt. This time, his voice emerged gently: "What's going on, please?"

Amber knew everything because Dick had told her and because her dad and Simp had told her too. She also knew Henry knew absolutely nothing. Amber dropped back down onto the couch, put her head into her hands, and started to cry harder. Dick was all she could think about. In a rush, she stuttered, "I-I think I love him! I do love him. It's only been— can you really be in love after two days? I can't help it. My dad's going to go mad."

Henry didn't know what he was expecting, but an open declaration of love from a strange girl who was decidedly not Petal wasn't it. He put his hands up to his face for half a second and hid behind his cupped palms, then he put them in his pockets. It was going to happen eventually: Dick would leave. And Henry only had to look at the girl on the couch to know the future was here and now. After what he'd been thinking about when he was in Dymchurch, it was almost a relief.

It had taken years of sorrow and anger at his loss before he'd understood the mistake he'd made by coming back. The bitterness he'd felt toward his own father was never resolved and it had carried over into the rest of his life. He'd lost good friends and a wife and made silly enemies, he'd turned from an openhearted, generous man into—well, he didn't know what. Sometimes he couldn't look at himself. The idea of Dick leaving him all alone scared him. From an early age, he'd more or less forced Dick to take over much of the farm's day-to-day running, hoping the responsibility would keep him at home. But not very deep down he knew Dick would leave, as he'd done in his day.

Henry swallowed and said, even more gently, "What's going on?"

For Amber that made things worse. She'd thought she didn't want to be shouted at, but sometimes a soft word was worse, much worse. Tears rolled, Amber grizzled. "I'm sorry, we—we just—it happened. It was like one of those films where people meet each other, like love at first sight. We couldn't help it..."

Although it went against the grain, Henry reached down and patted the girl's shoulder. His touch was warm and comforting and surprised them both. She looked up at him big-eyed.

Henry moved to an armchair opposite her and said, quietly, "Come on now, wipe your eyes. You'd best tell me what's going on. You and Dick and what?"

Tears were palmed away, sobs suppressed, as Amber tried to move things forward. "I told my dad where the bales were. It was stupid and I shouldn't have done it, like I knew it was wrong even as I told him, but he's my dad. Anyway, Dick and that other girl and a couple of others, they moved the stuff, and when Dad gets here and can't find it..."

Still in the dark, Henry scratched his beard. "I don't understand. What did they move? What's this about your dad? Bales of what? What's he after?"

That did it. Amber teetered. The truth hurt, but she didn't have anywhere else to go.

Henry sat back, amazed at his own uncharacteristic patience, as he waited for the full picture to emerge. He held his breath, because change was a strange thing. Life went on as though nothing would alter its direction, inertia ruled until it didn't. Then the whole world started to slip and slide. Here he was, sitting in his son's flat, a place he knew as well as he knew himself, but what he was looking at, when he looked at this girl, was something altogether new.

After she'd blown her nose, Amber told Henry everything. They went together down to the cellar and looked at the bales of grass. Amber told Henry what she remembered about the ferry and Petal's idea and about the meeting. Even as he looked at the bales of marijuana, it was hard to take it all in. This had all been going on and he'd known nothing. Enough elements of his ancestry were still in him, enough at least for him to visualize a time when smuggling was the family's trade and this cellar was stacked with wine, brandy, claret, and lace. Henry sat atop one of the bales and thought.

He thought about Amber and about Dick, he thought about the past, he thought about the future, he thought about his life on the island and what would happen when the ferry stopped, he thought about the law and the life his ancestors must have lived and how hard it must have been and the circumstances that had driven them to break the law of the land, he thought about Amber's dad and a bunch of thugs coming down to strong-arm himself and his neighbors. He thought it was time to stand up.

28

When Postmistress P had finished speaking, hands sprang up. Petal was ready. She waved her arms for a bit of quiet. "Okay, I've done a bit of research and I've got to say, it's all pretty boring stuff, so when you've had enough just tell me to shut up." She began to count the things she'd learned off on her fingers. "Right, cooperatives are owned and controlled by the members. That would be us, and everybody on the island would get a vote. We have to prepare a business plan. We have to choose something called a governing document, which would set out our co-op's rules. We need a name. We need to set up a bank account. We have to vote in directors, a chairperson, a secretary."

One of the blow-ins shouted, "All right, all right, enough already!"

There was laughter and Petal laughed too. "I told you it was boring. But there is one more thing." One arm in the air, a single finger pointing to the ceiling, she said, "We need a quorum!"

Probably 90 percent of the people there had absolutely no idea what a quorum was, but Julie started to giggle, Si had a big crooked grin on his chops, John Newman gave her the thumbs-up, and D.C. made silent clapping gestures. Postmistress P apart, most everybody else looked bemused.

Paloney and the vicar joined Petal at the head of the church, in front of the altar, ready to call for a vote, when

Henry Stick barged in through the closed church doors, Amber beside him. Heads turned. Everyone in the building knew Henry and everyone knew what he was like, a force of nature. Most winced. The rest goggled at Amber.

Without acknowledging a soul, Henry strode up the aisle. Before he reached the altar, he stopped and glanced behind him. Amber had come to a halt where Dick was sitting. They were touching hands and looking stupidly into each other's eyes. Henry came back and, taking Amber by the hand, said quickly to Dick, "Look, son, you two can sort things out later, but right now there are more important things and I need Amber."

Dick watched, stunned, mouth agape, as Amber and his father went hand in hand up the aisle. Petal gave Amber the pure evils as she and Henry stepped up. It was a pointless gesture. The church was crowded and there was so much going on in Amber's head, just standing there made her feel like a sacrificial lamb. All eyes were on her and it was like a moment in a film she'd seen, where a girl was made to stand on a box in front of some fundamental Christians and tell her sins.

Much to everyone's surprise, Henry shook hands with the vicar, Paloney, and Petal. As he shook Petal's hand, he said, "This whole co-op thing was your idea, right?"

Petal nodded. Henry smiled at her. Petal blinked back in surprise. She couldn't remember him smiling at her before, ever.

He said, "Good idea, very clever." and turning to Paloney, "Who knows about this?"

The policeman waved at the gathered people. "Well, we all know now. The whole island knows. In fact, we were just about to take a vote before you arrived."

Henry turned back to Petal. "Who found it in the first place?"

Petal sighed. Things weren't turning out quite as she had imagined. She nodded toward D.C. "Me, my dad, Si—" She paused and, with a twist in her voice, added, "And Dick."

Henry Stick looked over at his son, who shifted his eyes and gave his head a few ambiguous nods and shakes. Dick had no idea who that man was, impersonating his dad. As though there was only one answer to Dick's mystification, D.C. sparked up another spliff and passed it back to him.

For the first time in a long time, Henry had actually surprised people, even his son, and he didn't know why but he wanted to laugh. It felt good to surprise people. He asked, "What do we know about the people who're looking for the bales?"

Paloney said, "The only people who've had any real contact with them are D.C., Julian, and Penelope."

Henry gave a little laugh and pointed to Amber. "She may be able to help you there." Then, to Paloney, he asked, "What about your lot? Won't the police be after us?"

PC Paloney shook his head. "My superiors don't know anything about this. They won't catch us. They won't know unless someone tells them, and it won't be me."

On his feet again, D.C. offered, loudly, to take the blame. He thumped himself on the chest. "If a scapegoat is needed, I'm your man."

Not everyone believed him, but Julie and John stood beside him and, to everyone's surprise, Henry too.

Paloney shook his head. "Let's not go mad, this ain't a Spartacus situation."

To calm some of the people's fears of the law and prison, Julie and John offered to take responsibility for setting up the co-op and to put their names to the legal documents, if needed.

Henry clapped his hands to get attention. "Anyway, if we are going to go through with this, we better listen to what this young woman has to say." He reached down and gave her hand a little squeeze.

Amber looked out on the little world in front of her, coughed, stuttered, then said, "His name is Carter, he's my dad. I came down here to find out where the grass was hidden." She paused, and Dick's look of total shock rocked Amber. She felt her chin tremble, bit her lip and held hard. She'd done enough crying; now only the truth would work. "I told him where it was."

Dick's mouth opened and he shot forward in his seat, shaking his head in disbelief. Was he a complete fool! He'd taken Amber totally on face value, and now Petal was there shaking her head, a crooked little smile of triumph on her face. Dick didn't know if he was angry or hurt or humiliated. He made to speak but there were no words, and Amber kept her eyes on him as she continued: "He's planning to come down here tomorrow and take it back."

Silence ruled. Here was the crux, here was what it was all about. Stand or fall. No one spoke. Julian shuffled his feet, and Postmistress P said, "Not a very nice man, your dad, is he?"

It was true, but for Amber it seemed she'd said just enough bad things about her father and fancied a change. She said, "Depends who you are and what he wants."

Postmistress P laughed. "True enough of us all."

From near the back, a man said, "Anyway, he'll have a job. There isn't a ferry on a Sunday." That caused a little ripple of laughter.

Recognizing Tony from her journey over, she said, "That won't bother him. He'll pay you generously, and if you won't take money, he'll use force."

Tony said, "Him and that big fella?"

Flatly, Amber said, "There will be more of them this time."

Henry asked, "How many?"

Amber didn't know, so she guessed. "Four or five. He told me he'd have ten grand with him and it's take it or leave it, but he won't leave without the dope. Perhaps I could talk to him?"

Henry asked, "But from what you told me earlier, since it was moved, he doesn't know where it is, does he?"

Amber shook her head. "No."

Unable to stop herself, Petal pointed at the girl. "Why should we believe her? I don't trust her. She's already told him where the stuff was once. She saw us move it. All she needs to do is walk out of here and phone."

Dick spoke up. "Have you got a better idea?" Petal's face colored, and when she didn't answer, he snapped, "Well then."

Before an argument could start, Paloney interjected. "Anyway, the hardest thing we have to contend with will be getting the money."

Henry asked Amber, "How do we do that?" The girl was at a loss.

D.C. pulled a face. "That's the tricky bit."

Paloney said, "So what are you saying?"

Despite Petal's sneering look, Amber said, "Perhaps I could help. He'll expect me to meet him and take him to where it is." She paused. "I could talk to him."

Paloney gave her a sideways grin. "From what you said, he doesn't sound like a man who's coming to talk."

Amber wasn't sure but said, "Knowing Dad, he'll talk, until he can't get his own way."

Enough was enough. The policeman leaned over and whispered in Julian Crabbe's ear, and the vicar clapped his hands and addressed the congregation. "If we voted, say, on a show of hands and decide to accept the majority vote, would that seem reasonable?"

There were only two gainsayers. One, a very old man, didn't raise a hand because he hadn't any idea what was being said, and by the time it had been explained to him it didn't matter because the majority rules. The other was the woman Liz, with the two children. Julie asked what her objections were. Mostly it seemed to be on some kind of quasi-moralistic grounds, about drugs being bad. She said, "Is this the sort of thing we should involve ourselves in and what do we tell our children when they ask? What about the moral question?"

The moral question was too much for D.C. and he jumped up, exasperated. "Morally? There isn't a moral question involved."

She tried again: "But we'll be breaking the law. What will happen if they catch us?"

Before Paloney had to repeat himself, D.C. waved a hand in his own direction. "Me. I already said I'll take the blame and Paloney already told us he's the law here. Also, there is a difference between morality and the law. So let's get beyond what the cargo is. All right, some of you don't take drugs and some of you don't even like the idea of other people taking drugs. Fair enough. But try to think of it as merely a product, you know, like beans—and if we had a hill of beans turn up on the beach and we found a buyer, would it be wrong to sell the beans?" He held out his hands in supplication to the woman. "Come on, really? It's like finding some lost hoard of Saxon coins or something, what do they call it?"

Paloney said, "A treasure trove."

D.C. nodded. "Yeh, thanks! It's like that, except we don't have to offer ours to the government before we can spend it."

Liz sighed heavily and said, testily, "I'm not happy, but I accept the majority decision. I want to stay on the island as much as the next person—I was only asking. I just don't think we should have to break the law to do it."

A spoiler plan for Carter was formed and the meeting ended. A bit later, outside the church, where a lot of the islanders were hanging around, talking the whole situation over, Paloney, police hat under his arm, finally took the spliff from D.C. After a long drag he said, "Thank heavens that's over."

D.C. put a hand on his friend's shoulder. "Yeh, but tomorrow's coming."

Off to one side by themselves, Amber and Dick went through a little litany of accusation and apology. Dick dismayed, Amber contrite. But none of that could last for very long. They moved to each other slowly and near to each other such that they couldn't help touching; little gestures and looks, and love wasn't dead. Dick reasoned, whatever her original intentions, Amber had come good and the past was the past and love still existed. Amber felt a little spaced out, like she'd gone through some kind of trial. Deception had been stripped away and she had chosen a side. The only worry was it wasn't her dad's side. They kissed, it was good.

Henry was happy. He didn't know exactly why, but he didn't care either. Something had slipped away, like when people say a weight had been lifted off their shoulders, but what he felt was more abstract. He spoke to people and shook hands with folks he wouldn't normally acknowledge, and it was nice when people said, "Nice one, H," or "Way to go, Henry." What could he do but smile and say thank you? He'd shaken hands with John Newman for the first time in nearly twenty years. He felt all strange and open. It was a sensation he'd forgotten.

He couldn't explain why the world had turned when he'd looked at Amber earlier that evening, but it had and he'd known, in an instant, Dick was as good as gone. It was a flash and the world had turned. It was what Henry wanted, needed, and he hadn't known it completely until that moment. The idea made him smile. Suddenly the farm, the bane of his adult life, his chosen burden for years, didn't matter. As they walked to the Land Rover, he put his arms around Dick's and Amber's shoulders and said, "This is the most exciting thing to happen here in..." But he couldn't think of an *in*, so he said, "There's cold cider in the fridge. Why don't we go back to the house and talk about the future?"

Sometimes it takes time to get around to things, and the three of them sat at the kitchen table drinking ice-cold cider.

One, two, three glasses. Henry raised his chin toward Amber. "You've got a good girl here, boy."

Dick was in a kind of semi-shocked-type state. It was like suddenly the real man had stepped out from behind the man. Dick was stunned and it wasn't over.

Henry poured more cider. "I've been stupid. I'm sorry. I'm going over to see John Newman tomorrow. It's been a long time coming, but think I'm going to say sorry to him. When we were your age, we were best friends, like you and Si."

He paused and they all drank more cider, starting to get a bit pissed. Henry was on a roll, so he said, carefully, "You're going to leave." He waved at Amber. "And who wouldn't."

It was all too much for Dick, he couldn't believe it. He did a double take on his dad to give himself time, then he said, slowly, almost warily, "I would like to leave, but I know how things are and, anyway, I don't have anywhere to stay or any money."

Henry looked at Dick and Amber across the table. He felt soft and daft and quite peaceful. He was breathing easy. He said, "Why don't you go and stay with your mother until you sort things out."

Pushing himself up from the table, Henry shambled from the room. They could hear him clumping about upstairs and pulled faces at each other and wondered whatever would happen next. After a few minutes, he returned and slapped a post office savings book on the table and pushed it toward Dick. He watched the sudden look of shock as it flitted across his son's face as he open the savings book.

"Dad, this—this is thousands."

A surprise still to himself, Henry smiled. "I've been putting a bit away for you for a few years now. You won't starve. Enough to set yourself up in..." He stopped, having absolutely no idea what Dick wanted to do. He shrugged. "Whatever you want."

Dick shook his head. All the excuses he'd had for staying on the island, for staying safe, for dreaming rather than taking action, were gone. It was strange, overwhelming. Confused, he said, "But what about you? I can't leave you alone on the farm."

Henry studied the lino at his feet and then looked up at Dick. There were tears in his eyes. "Son, sod the farm! Don't make the same mistake I did. I'll look for someone with a few bob to invest, a partner or someone to help take the load." Henry shrugged and stood up from the kitchen table. "It's all change, son. You, me, the farm—all change. Anyway, I'm going to have a piss." He waved a hand at Amber. "Sorry, don't mind my language."

When he'd gone, Amber whispered, "Your dad's lovely. He was so nice to me earlier."

Stunned by his father's sudden metamorphoses into Mr. Nice Guy, Dick laughed out loud. His dad being lovely. That was a first. He'd heard his father called many things over the years but lovely wasn't one of them. He said, "What's happened? What have you done? What did you say to him? I don't remember him being like this since I was a little kid. It's fantastic."

Amber blushed. "I-I don't know, I just told him the truth. I was scared at first but he was nice, he listened."

To Dick, it seemed his world had turned upside down in a couple days. All the impossibilities had become possibilities. It was all almost too much to take, and it made Dick giggle some more. He shook his head in complete admiration. "You're lovely, Amber. Thank you."

29

Henry sat at the kitchen table for a good while after Dick and Amber had shuffled off to the flat. He still felt strange and a little elated and not ready for sleep. He walked out into the garden at the front of the house. The grass was long and the rosebushes were blown and half covered in rank, climbing reeds. He pulled down his fly and leisurely pissed on the nearest one.

All about him was quiet, and Henry took long, slow breaths. He hadn't felt so relaxed in years. For once, he didn't resent the farm or the island. He glanced about at the old house and garden, at the tall trees all shadowy and dark, and he looked out beyond, to all the places he couldn't see, all the acres of the farm and the low-slung black lump of the island, and he felt good.

Back in the house, he took a fresh quart of cider from the fridge and walked back through the garden and out onto the road. It was near midnight, and the moon dropped light, fitful and random, through the shifting clouds. Henry mooched about, sipping cider, with no particular place to go. As he entered the village, he was surprised to see a beaten-up Morris Minor parked beside the phone box. There were two kids asleep in baby seats in the back, and Liz was on the phone.

Since his wife left him, Henry had had few affairs and even fewer with women on the island. Liz had been one of the few, and somehow they were still, ten years on, almost friends. She'd turned up one summer, before D.C. and the rest of the wasters. It had been easy to tell she didn't come from the laboring classes, but she'd worked in the fields with the rest. It had also been obvious, back then, she was fragile, and while they were lovers she'd told him she'd had a nervous break-down while at university—a culmination of years pandering to overbearing parents whom, she'd claimed, she never want-ed to see again. Sensitive as she was, it had amazed Henry they had ever managed to get together, and their affair lasted but the one summer.

Liz had stayed on. To Henry, a shadow of that fragility had stayed on with her as well. A few years later, she had hooked up with Terry Davis, one of the island's more useless residents. They were together for a while, but after the second of the two chavvies made an entrance, Terry had quit the island. Some said he was working on the rigs off Aberdeen.

Without thinking much about it, Henry pulled open the phone box door, and Liz jumped and the handful of coins from her hand spilled to the floor. She stared at him, bug-eyed. "What do you want? What are you doing here—are you drunk?"

Surprised, Henry pulled back but kept a hand on the open door. "Me? Nothing. I saw you and just thought I'd say hello."

She squatted to gather up the coinage. "Hello? You must be drunk, wandering around in the middle of the night."

Henry laughed. "Maybe, but what are you doing this time of night? Who are you phoning? Not Terry, surely?"

Liz swung her head back and forth, like a heifer awaiting slaughter, as she counted the cash. "We don't speak anymore."

Unable to help himself, Henry said, "With luck, he'll never come back."

Straightening up, Liz gave him a look he couldn't read, but there were tears in her eyes. "I wasn't phoning him. I don't even know where he is."

There must have been near a quid in Liz's palm—it wasn't a local call. Henry drank a little cider and thought about the way she voted. He passed the bottle to Liz; she palmed it off. Henry joked, "Who you phoning, then?"

She didn't answer for a few seconds, then said, "I was surprised at you tonight, the way you voted."

Henry had been surprised himself for hours on end now, and he shrugged and drank. "I think I voted for the best."

Liz was unhappy, weighed down, and it had been hard lately to think straight. The boys didn't help. In a dark part of her, she wanted to smash something, to go as she had in her teens, off the rails. Unhappily, she admitted, "I said I'd go along with the majority, but I can't, I think it's wrong. It's not the drugs—well, not altogether." She gestured toward the car. "I've got two young children." She spoke as though it was some kind of truth, some baseline that everybody understood. In case Henry was too drunk to comprehend, she added, "No one should have to rely on criminality to survive, not in a country like this. It corrupts us all, even the innocents. If you must know, I was going to phone the police."

Henry did not immediately react to this. He was the man, after all, who'd created a row until a policeman had finally been posted to the island, when it hadn't had one for years. They sent Paloney, and whatever he'd thought before, he'd come to realize the man was perfect for the island. Finally, he smirked, "Come on, Liz, if the real police come here, half the island could be arrested for something." He stopped, then said, "Even you."

That got her. She bridled. "What do you mean? I've done nothing. I'm doing nothing. What are you talking about?"

Henry looked sideways, he drank some cider, he looked up at the sky, and he pointed at the car. "Don't take this wrong, Liz, but I know your car's not legal." Before she could reply, he added, with a grin, "Even Paloney knows your car ain't legal."

It was true. Liz opened and closed her hand over the money and started to cry. She could barely keep the basics together anymore. She said, "I don't know what to do, Henry."

He put a comforting hand on her shoulder. He didn't want her to phone the police, but a little bit drunk, he didn't know what to do either and so went for a simple drunk's answer. "Look, Liz, why don't you go home. Here." He shoved the half-full bottle of cider into her hand. "Drive the kids home and put them to bed, have a little drink and think about it. Sleep on it, think about everybody else."

Liz took the bottle. She was fed up with thinking of other people. "I know Terry was..." She shook her head. "It's not been easy. To be honest, I don't want to think about anything anymore. I like you, Henry, but I don't know, I'm scared for the future."

30

Once he'd decided on a course of action, Carter liked to get things done. They set out early, Carter and Simp in the BMW and the other four stooges following behind in the panel van. What he actually felt, no one but Carter knew. To Simp everything Carter did was a confidence-building exercise. It was bluster, ego, arrogance. Carter was in charge and he liked to show it, in the way he flexed his shoulders, in the deep brown luster of his brogues, the way he adjusted the jacket of his dark maroon mohair suit, the way he darted his head forward and pulled at the cuffs of his shirt. The way he talked to the thugs in the van. The way he relaxed back into the seat of the car as it shot through the long stretches of London's sprawling suburbia, out into the green of the Kent countryside. A little king in his world.

They settled into the drive. Simp jabbed a tape into the deck. Another soul compilation. Wilson Pickett went by and then Sam Cooke. When Gladys Knight came on singing "Midnight Train to Georgia," Carter gave an obnoxious laugh. "Will you listen to this? Fuck me, what a fucking bunch of shite! Listen to her. Sitting there with her poncy L.A. mates and slagging off her bloke." Mockingly, Carter started to sing along to certain lyrics: *"L.A. proved too much for the man. He couldn't make it... he's going back to... the world he left behind."* He reached into the inside pocket of his jacket, took his flask out, and, looking at Simp in defiance, took a long snifter. "What a horrible song. Basically, she's saying he can't cut the custard, and all her mates, those snide fuckers, singing in the back, *Oh, ah, and he didn't get far.* What the fuck? Listen, she sings, *So he pawned all his hopes and even sold his old car.*" Carter jabbed a finger at Simp. "She even puts him down because he doesn't have a good motor. Oh, yeh, and then she tells her mates she's going." Carter warbled, *"And I'll be with him."* He took another shot from the flask. "Like he's a complete tosser, but what can a girl do? She loves him. Then there's her friends, *we know you will, we're sure you will,* like she's some kind of martyr. A bunch of snide fuckers. So tell me, soul man, what kind of a two-faced cunt is she, eh? Who'd want to go anywhere with her?" He slumped back into his seat and expelled a great lungful of air. Simp handed him a couple of tablets. Carter took them and washed them down with another snort.

Simp looked at him sideways and sighed. Still building himself up. Simp had seen it all before. If it wasn't "Midnight Train to Georgia," it would be something else to gee up the nervous system. He'd been with Carter since forever, but everything changes, sometimes slowly, and sometimes it is just the end, over. This was both. Ideas had been simmering in Simp's head from before they came to the island. Simp had been looking at himself, at the future. He was creeping past forty. He'd done well financially, but the future for someone with his particular skill set didn't get better as you got older. The island was like the glimpse of another world. Carter didn't see it. Couldn't see either that they'd both got away with it for an awful long time, that they had been lucky, and how much money does anyone need, anyway? He drove and said nothing. He'd attempted, more than once, to talk Carter out of the confrontation he was sure they were heading into. "Pay them," he'd said. "Just give them the money, we won't lose out." Carter's response had been the usual "Money's money. I ain't giving it away to them or anyone." Simp didn't want to go down to the island and hurt anyone. He'd reached a point where he was getting sick of it. Carter, the business, all of it.

At Dymchurch they found the ferrymen, Tony and his son, Dave, lounging on the dock. At first, Carter couldn't believe the ferry didn't run on a Sunday. He puffed out his chest and strode about. "Typical, leave the Smoke and it's like going back a fucking hundred years!"

The ferrymen were unmoved by the differences between city and country and talked instead about the difficulties involved in moving the ferry. They muttered on about their license being revoked if they were reported, about their need for a rest day, but didn't say no way. They quibbled and groused and scratched their heads and picked their teeth, and in the end, it cost Carter five hundred quid. Before they got going, Dave popped into their house and phoned Postmistress P, who alerted the waiting islanders.

They tied up at the island dock and the BMW and the panel van trundled off. Carter was expecting Amber to be waiting. When she wasn't, they turned slowly onto the village street. It was deserted. The two vehicles crawled slowly along. Outside the post office, Carter, as though he were Ward Bond from *Wagon Train*, held a hand up out of the car window and called a halt. Carter and Simp got out and Carter peered through the shop window into the darkened interior.

Simp said, "It's Sunday, it's closed."

Carter said, "I fucking know that, don't I?" Still, he reached for the door handle and began to rattle it. To both their surprise, the handle turned and the door swung open. It was cool and dim inside the shop, smelling of cleaning fluid and dry pet food and something else both recognized. They inched forward, hunched, ready for an ambush. Nothing happened.

At the post office counter, on the scales, weighing in at exactly half a pound, was a brown paper package tied up with string. Neither Carter nor Simp needed to be told what it held, the smell was enough. Carter reached down, pulled up the leg of his trousers, took the Stanley knife from the sheath strapped to his calf, and cut the string. Inside the packet was a pile of his own grass. He kicked out at the base of the counter. "What's this? What are they doing? Where the fuck is Amber?"

Simp shrugged. "Are these like more of those rhetorical questions? Because if they are like real questions, then I don't know."

Stalking toward the door, the package under his arm, Carter snapped, "Shut up with that shit. Something's wrong, something's always wrong on this fucking island."

Outside, Carter went to the panel van. The driver rolled down the window as he approached. "What's going on, boss?"

Thrusting the package of grass into the man's hand, Carter slowly shook his head, like he was surrounded by idiots. "How the fuck do you expect me to know, you twat? I got here the same time as you. Now, look after this."

Leaving the vehicles and the men where they were, Simp and Carter walked the few yards to the vicar's house. Carter's eyes were beginning to itch. He rubbed them and blinked. He said, "If he's in there, I'm bringing him with us."

Simp sighed. "I thought you never wanted to see him again after last time."

Carter looked down at himself. He touched the lapels of the suit, straightened the skinny tie, and continued: "Like a bargaining chip, you know? Who wants to see their dill of a rev hurt, eh? Nobody, not even this bunch of fucking heathens."

The door was ajar. Inside all was quiet. On the table in the living room were a pack of cards and another package of grass. Hardly calm, Carter rushed through the house, up and down and in every room. Empty. While he was gone, Simp got a glass of water from the kitchen and a couple of the pills from his pocket, and when Carter came back into the living room, he handed the medication to his boss. Pushing the glass of water aside, Carter pulled his flask from his pocket and swallowed the pills with a long hit of whiskey.

Back on the village street again, Carter handed the grass into the van. Under his breath, one of the guys said, "It's going to take years to collect it like this."

Carter stuck his head through the van window. "What did you say?"

The man held up his hands. "Nothing, boss, nothing."

Back in the car with Simp, Carter said, "What do these carrot crunchers think this is, a fucking treasure hunt?"

The mini-convoy trundled on to the church, where it stopped again. The church doors were wide open. Simp said, "Maybe he's in the church." For some reason, the wide-open doors made Carter a tad more nervous than anything else. This time he called the four men from the van, and the six of them entered the church together, mob handed.

It was all cool and airy and empty, and the men stood there, looking at the bare whitewashed walls, the aged wooden pews, the cross and its bloody burden, the unpretentious altar. Quietly, Simp said, "First time I've been in church for years. It's kind of nice in here, peaceful."

Carter gave Simp a disbelieving look. "What's the matter with you, you going soft or something?"

It wasn't worth Simp answering. Instead, leaving the other goondas standing there like a bunch of plonkers with brain damage, Simp followed Carter up the nave to the altar. It wasn't much of a surprise to see the brown paper parcel, foursquare, where the Bible would usually be. Carter slammed his fist down on the altar. He wanted to desecrate: burn, smash, whatever. It was in his eyes, in the set of his shoulders, the jerking movements of his body. Simp could see it all. Almost gently, he put his arm around Carter and led him from the church.

Outside, Simp tried again to remonstrate with Carter, to get him to see reason, but it was useless and his temper only got worse, as they noticed a front tire on each of the vehicles had been punctured while they had been inside, and it didn't help that Carter's sinuses were becoming blocked and his eyes, gummed and rheumy. Simp offered antihistamines. Carter slapped them away. "I don't need them. I don't need anything."

It took almost forty minutes to change the two wheels and, as if trying to wear a trough in the asphalt, Carter marched back and forth, back and forth, the whole time, wondering what the fuck had happened to Amber. Finally, the caravan started up again, and Carter and Simp followed Amber's instructions to the farm, where the dope was supposedly being kept. It wasn't hard. Both remembered the track down to the bay and the farm they had passed on the way. It was made easier for them by the packet of grass taped to the open farm gate. In the yard, two of the goons pulled back the big double doors to the barn. A solitary sheep rushed out of the dark interior and, blinded by the sudden sunlight, careened helter-skelter full into Carter, tossing him to the ground. That was the ultimate indignity. He didn't like people much, but animals, animals were less than nothing, and to be upended by a fucking sheep was more than he could stand. There was a packet taped to its back, and the goons chased it back into the barn, where they cornered it, allowing Carter to run up and kick it in the head. The animal gave a solitary bleat and fell to its knees, stunned. The barn was empty.

Where was Amber? That was what Carter wanted to know. Of all the things that were happening, that was what bothered him the most. They looked around the empty barn, at a loss for what to do next. He turned to Simp. "What have they done to her?"

Simp was a patient man, up to a point, and now he'd had enough. "Boss, I don't think they've done anything to her. Like I told you, it's wrong. It feels wrong. I don't like it. The truth is you're wrong. Give them the money."

Carter couldn't believe what he was hearing. It was like some play he'd heard about, where the mates of some emperor or other had all turned around and stabbed him at once. "You're saying she's played me?" Simp shrugged apologetically, but Carter couldn't take it. His head hurt. His eyes hurt. His lungs hurt. He rounded on Simp. "Wrong! Wrong! That's all I ever hear from you and that daughter of mine. Wrong! I'm in fucking charge, do you get me? Me. That's enough already. Right, wrong, what the fuck has it got to do with you?"

Simp was a big man, and suddenly, in the semidarkness of the barn, he loomed over Carter. He spoke quietly. "What's it got to do with me? It's got everything to do with me. It's my bloody life. I've been thinking lately, and you know what? I've nearly had enough of this, boss. We're getting older. I've been with you through everything, but..." Simp paused, collected himself. "But you carry on with this and we could be done now, do you get me?"

There was nothing more to say. Argument unresolved, the two went back to the car. There was no changing Carter.

Still convinced he could sort it for ten grand, Carter said, "Let's go back to the village, see if we can find someone."

As they pulled out of the yard, Simp punched in his favorite soul tape. "Me and Mrs. Jones" came on. Carter reached out to turn it off. Simp dropped a hand from the steering wheel and swiped him away. With no other recourse, Carter took out his flask and had a long drink.

Just before the turn into the village, they were forced to slow, thanks to a tractor that had been parked sideways across the lane, making it impassable. Carter's head fell to his chest, and he muttered, "These fuckers think they're clever, trying to spook us."

"There's a lot more of them than us," Simp said cryptically, leaving Carter with that thought as he got out of the car and went back to the van. "Back up into the yard again, lads. We'll turn around and you follow us." Back in the car, he said, "Better pull yourself together, boss."

Carter sighed and tried as best he could to take deep breaths.

Simp said, "Remember, if we follow this lane toward that bay and then keep going, we end up back at the ferry."

Straightening his shoulders, Carter nodded.

By the time they came in sight of the ferry, Carter'd had a couple of shots. Maybe the pollen count was down, because the hay fever seemed to have abated, but maybe, anyway, it was just the ozone up his snozz had cleared it out. Regardless, when they got to the bay, Simp insisted they stop. Carter didn't argue, because underneath it all, with him and Simp, some part of it was as deep as the love he felt for Amber, though he'd never tell. He didn't know what he would do without him. Already, he'd readjusted everything Simp had said into the fact that he, Carter, shouldn't fuck around with his music, and all right, he, Carter, could live with that.

Simp had got all the goons out and took them for a stroll on the beach. Even Carter went. It was strange and, if you liked nothing ever happening but a few clouds and sea and stuff, even Carter thought it was all right. Anyway, the boys seemed to like it, stupid big tossers. It perked them up. In fact, if he knew what Amber was about, and he got his dope back, everything would be perfick.

The two ferrymen were sat on the dock. As they turned onto the village's main street, unable to help himself, Carter gave a nonchalant wave.

Outside the post office the road was blocked double deep by islanders. Not everybody was out—Henry Stick noticed Liz was absent—but there was a smattering of old blokes, the odd granny, a mess of hippies and proto-crusties (all dreads and post-punk bullshit), a pair of Mrs. Blue Raincoats, bug-eyed, dragged there by their slightly wayward teenage offspring. There were local guys with blackthorn sticks, blow-ins with mullets, and dogs on string, mothers and fathers with the kids in their arms and others strapped into strollers. On the front line was Julie, D.C., the vicar, Postmistress P, John Newman, Henry Stick, Si, Petal, PC Paloney in uniform, and, there in the middle, Amber holding hands with Dick. Beyond them all, a tractor and high-sided trailer blocked the street.

Carter and Simp sat in the car and looked. What was Amber doing, standing there with the carrot crunchers, and who in hell was the green-haired guy she was holding hands with? He looked like a dill. Then Tony and Dave walked past the car, smiled, waved, and went to join the crowd. Five hundred quid didn't buy loyalty. Nothing bought loyalty.

Carter thought about his daughter and thought about Simp, and he remembered what he wanted and forgot the rest, and although Simp didn't show it, he was exasperated. He said, calmly, "Look, boss, you can't fight a whole island. Why don't we just give them what they want? There's still plenty of money to be made—remember, you don't have to pay the Colombians."

Sometimes that word was like a switch, and Carter could hardly contain himself: "Don't talk money to me! What the fuck do you know? I'll give them what they need all right, but it won't be what they want!"

Confrontation was Carter's favorite way to deal with the world. He stepped out of the car. He looked good and he knew it. It helped. Looking good could change the day. He tried a smile—it didn't really work—but one brush down with the hands and the suit looked perfect: three buttons, slim lapels, hand stitched (naturally), eight-inch side vents, five-button cuffs, ticket pocket, timeless. All his suits were similar. He set his shoulders.

Reluctantly Simp followed and stood next to his boss. The four men in the van climbed out and stood alongside Carter and Simp. They each had a baseball bat. Carter straightened his slim tie at the knot and gave the onlookers a bit of a static shoulder swagger, just to let the people know who was boss. He took a good lungful of sweet, warm, oxygenated pollen. It tickled at the back of his throat.

As he stood there, Simp felt strange, uncomfortable, on the verge of something. If Carter set his mind to it, he could easily get what he wanted from most people with bribes, and if not, then he could go where others wouldn't go, with violence. With Carter, it mostly went the latter way. That was the trouble, and that had been Carter and Simp at work for years. Trouble was Simp didn't enjoy it anymore.

Carter reached in the car and pulled out a black cotton drawstring bag and threw it into the no-man's-land between himself and the islanders. "Here, that's ten grand, take it or leave it. I don't want any trouble, I just want my product back." He waved an arm at the gathered motley crew and said disparagingly, "You lot think you can stop me, but you're just a bunch of fucking yokels and we'll run straight through you." By the time he'd finished speaking his voice had risen and his eyes were popping. A number of the villagers stepped back a pace and the four men with baseball bats stepped forward a pace.

Simp didn't move but whispered in Carter's ear, "I don't want to do this. Anyway, there's only the five of us."

Breathing raggedly and red-faced now, Carter shook his head and sneered. "It ain't about what you want to do!" He coughed. Something was wrong.

Leaving Dick's hand behind, Amber stepped forward. Her dad didn't look well; his face was tomato red. She didn't want to feel sorry for him, not right now, but he was still her dad. Amber knew, mostly, you couldn't reason with him, but she tried anyway. "Daddy, you don't have to do this, you don't have to be like this. Almost everyone here knows now how much that cargo is worth. Ten grand ain't going to work. Even if you pay them what they want, you can't lose. These people are trying to save their homes and livelihoods. Come on, Dad."

Carter's face itched. He pulled out a handkerchief and blew his nose. Simp looked over at Amber and the rest of the islanders. Amber gave him a surreptitious little wave and smiled. Simp pulled a don't-know face but, feeling moody, tried Carter again. "You know, boss, what Amber said is right, you'll still make plenty of money."

Carter turned on Simp. "I told you, it's not up to you"—he threw out an arm and pointed toward his daughter—"or her. I ain't a charity. Do you get me? There's ten grand on the road there, you all can take it or leave it, but we don't leave here without my product."

Amber wanted to go to him, to hug and show him love, and she would have done it if, even in her wildest dreams, she thought it would make a difference. Instead, she took a backward step and picked up Dick's hand.

Carter's breath came heavy then and he started to sniff and sneeze, to cough and choke. In the hedgerow, the flower heads of the sukebind gently waved. Simp went to the car and took a strip of pills from the glove compartment. "Here. Antihistamine." Carter was red-eyed, red-faced, beginning to bloat. He ripped a couple of tabs from the strip and threw them into his mouth. It had never been so bad. From across the divide, he heard the whisper: "Sukebind fever." What the fuck was that? He punched two more tabs out and necked them.

Everybody, including the sukebind, watched fascinated as he crunched, swallowed, and almost choked again, as the pills caught in his throat. Simp slapped him on the back. Carter hated weakness and hated himself when it showed. He took out the flask and had a swallow. He breathed slow and long. It seemed the older he got, the more sensitive he became. When he had control, Carter said to Simp, "Let's get in the vehicles and just drive straight through them." Simp said nothing. The tractor and trailer were obvious. To the islanders, Carter said, "You stupid fuckers. We know exactly where it is. She may be standing with you, but she's my daughter. Now get out of the fucking way or we'll run you down." He tried to laugh but stopped, as it bent in his throat into a cough.

The vicar coughed too and then said, "You know it's not there, we know it's not there. Why bother to lie?"

There are moments when the same old nonsense won't wash anymore, and Simp was at the finish line. It was over. Although he didn't know what he wanted, he wanted something else. It was done. Sometimes it's like that. Flatly, he said, "I ain't doing it."

Carter couldn't believe it. All the years and all the money. What the fuck was happening? Loyalty? Obviously didn't mean shit. Didn't him and Simp go beyond loyalty? Back to the day before the day. And Amber? She was his daughter. He'd given her everything he'd never had and she was standing there with the fucking enemy. He could feel something coming on and it wasn't nice.

Out of the game, Simp put his fists in his pockets the way another may holster a gun or sheath a knife and eyed the folks opposite. They were just a bunch of ordinary people and he didn't have the heart for it. On the front line there was a man, a big fella like himself, but older. They looked each other up and down. Simp nodded and the other man lifted his chin in acknowledgment. There wasn't anything to say to someone like Carter, because he would never understand, so Simp didn't say good-bye; instead he slowly crossed the no-man's-land and stood uncertainly in front of Henry Stick. He said, "Hit me, I need some pain."

Not at all sure, Henry made a fist and weighed it in the air. Both men looked at it. Henry said, "Look, I'm trying to change my ways."

Simp grinned. "Me too." He held out a hand, and tentatively the two men shook. Simp said, "All right? My name's Simon."

Carter couldn't believe his eyes. He blinked. Sure, they'd had rows before, but they had always sorted them out. Simp? What was this?

Then D.C. laughed out loud. "You can drive through us, but how are you going to get back?" The ferry guys were laughing behind their hands.

A cheeky teen yelled, "Didn't anyone tell you there isn't a return ferry on a Sunday?"

The rest of the islanders began to titter, giggle, chortle, and smirk. Simp kept a straight face.

The four thugs hefted their baseball bats but looked perplexed, and Carter looked like a volcano on the verge of eruption. His face was purple. His hands carved and slashed at the air. He'd heard about people crossing the Rubicon and had never understood what it meant; now he knew. Even though he still didn't know what a Rubicon was, Simp had definitely crossed it.

Watching her father made Amber cringe. She wanted to run over to him, stop him from humiliating himself. Again she tried to reason with him. "Look, Dad, I know you don't like to compromise, but really, crumbs, Dad, you told me. The South Americans have already written off their loss."

No, no, no, Carter wasn't going to have that, wasn't going to have his business talked about in front of anybody, let alone a bunch of fucking carrot crunchers. His own daughter and Simp. What were they doing?! Simp. It was all wrong. What had he ever done to either of them that they could treat him this way? Leave him when he needed them most. Enough already.

In the slim sheath strapped to his calf, Carter had the Stanley knife, taped up so only half an inch of blade showed. His favorite weapon. It left a smile or opened an artery, depending. He swung it backward and forward in an arc in front of him. "Come on, come on, step up. I'll take any of you on. Let's settle this man-to-man."

Postmistress P didn't wait but, like a dervish, spun out from the crowd, and with one deft kick she sent the Stanley knife somersaulting off across the road. Before Carter could react, she landed a short hook to the kidneys and, as he folded, a punch to the side of his head that sent him down.

There were gasps and a closing of gaps in the line, and Julian Crabbe grinned, wide-eyed. Some woman. She always had something else. He loved it that she never explained what she'd got up to before she came back to the island. It was a bit like playing love poker. For some reason, as the islanders shuffled together, they linked arms, tic-tak-tok, like chorus girls, and straggled forward, and Julian went with them, smiling, happy to be part of everything. The thugs looked at one another. They moved away, back toward the van, even though there was no place to go when they got there. They didn't look at Carter.

The man himself was crouched down, squealing and banging his head on the ground. No one moved now. Nothing happened. Motion snapped into tableau. Most eyes watched. A soft wind blew. The sun shortened the shadows. Birds twittered in trees. A dog barked. The sukebind rustled. Postmistress P was still poised, ready to strike again. It lasted and lasted, and each moment was pure pain to both Simp and

Amber. She didn't know what to do; she had never seen her father like this before and she didn't know who she should be more scared for, the islanders or her dad. She'd seen him angry, raging, but this was something else. She wanted to rush over but was rooted, wide-eyed with shock, to the spot. Simp looked along the line of islanders at Amber. He may have left Carter, but it was more than he could bear to have Amber watch her father implode. They almost moved together, daughter, friend. Carter was lucky to have them.

Only Simp really knew about Carter and why he always carried the pills with him. Carter's trouble was he wanted to kill everybody and he knew he couldn't. That was what the hurt and rage were. Simp took the bottle of pills out, shook a couple into his hand, and went over to the man. What else could he do? They both knelt beside Carter, because there was no one else to hug the man and to stop him smashing his head onto the road. Both Amber and Simp patted him and crooned to him, cooed him gently into quiet. Simp fed him his pills for the last time and slipped the bottle into Carter's jacket pocket. It was over.

When Simp got fed up with the crying on his shoulder, Amber took over, and in the end all three squatted down and held one another, sobbing...

31

Henry wasn't much for intuition. He'd never had a presentiment, but something sent him to the dock Monday morning. Liz had been so sad the other night, Henry didn't think a half quart of cider was going to cure it. It was a gray day, still and cool. Sheets of thin dull clouds covered the sky. Tiny wavelets slapped the dockside. The ferry rode easy at its mooring. School was out for the summer holidays, and without the chattering flock of children, the dockside was quiet.

There waiting, kids strapped into a stroller, was Liz. He walked beside her onto the ferry and said, "Are you going to the police?"

Head down, Liz nodded. A moment later, she said, "Why don't you leave me alone?"

With a nod toward the stroller, he said, "I see you've left the car at home—no tax and no insurance don't go down well on the mainland."

That little threat may have worked the previous night, but now she just looked at him and pursed her lips.

When the ferry cast off, they stood looking back at the island. Finally Henry said, "I know you have your reasons, and at other times, I would probably agree with you, but—"

Liz cut him off. "Why not this time? You've always been against the way the island is changing."

He didn't have the words to explain, so instead he pulled a couple of faces that told her nothing and said, "I don't know, but this feels different. It's not just about you and me—the whole island is under threat. Selling that man Carter back his drugs won't hurt your children. Come on, Liz, they are too young to notice, and by the time they are old enough to understand, it will have become folklore, like the wrecking and the smuggling."

They stood resting against the safety rail at the back of the ferry. The sea was flat and green, the wake white. Seagulls flew high and suddenly dipped low and skimmed the trail of foam before wheeling back up into the sky.

Henry said, "You know, when my ancestors came here nine hundred years ago, we owned everything: land, surf, cows, sheep, rabbits. We owned the herrings in the sea." He laughed. "We took bounty from everything, living and dead. If you pulled a fish from the sea, we took a fillet." Liz cracked a half smile. Henry said, "Look at me now. Times change."

With a jab of cruelty, she replied, "You're strange, Henry, what do you want me to say? Poor you, how the mighty have fallen."

"That's not what I'm on about. I was thinking of you and your lads. This is your and their home. Who knows what the future will bring? You left everything—university, the chance of a proper job—you walked out on your own parents and ended up here. You don't really want to leave, do you?" They watched the island shrink slowly, green, lush, beautiful. Henry said, "Do you remember when your Ben was born? Your parents came over for the christening. It was the first time you'd seen them in years. They didn't take to Terry, but you can't blame them for that. They didn't agree with the way you lived and they didn't like the island. As I recall, they tried to force you to go back with them to the family home. You wouldn't go and they didn't come back for the second christening."

Liz couldn't help it, tears started in the corners of her eyes. She squatted down, her face hidden, and fussed at the boys and the blanket on the double buggy. One, untroubled, sucked his thumb; the other slept, head on one side. Eyes still misty, Liz stood up slowly. "Like I said, it's not just the drugs, it's me. I want something to happen, something to change the direction of my life. If I go to the police, everybody on Stickle will hate me and I'll have to do something about myself. Leave, something."

At a loss for an answer, Henry said, "Not everybody will hate you."

Liz began to sob again.

As though comforting crying women had become an everyday thing, he put his arm across her shoulders. "And like I said, if we don't do this the island is finished. Now tell me truthfully, do you really want to do this, turn your back on ten years of your life? Isn't there something, some way—"

She interrupted him by blowing her nose. "I know Terry was useless, but it's hard on my own. I'm worn out, Henry. I'm sick of struggling on the dole. I love my boys, but bringing up young kids is basically boring, it's tedious, I go for days without talking to another adult. The cottage is damp and hard to heat and impossible to keep clean."

Henry pulled her a bit closer and patted her back. He understood what she meant about the kids—he'd done it with Dick, but at least he'd had the distraction of the farm, he'd been able to take the boy about the place with him and afford a babysitter when he needed to get away. He also understood about life closing in, the frustration, the sense of being trapped, and he remembered the years of pointless anger, the strife and arguments he'd caused, the stupid things he'd done. Now he tried to fathom a way out for Liz and the island.

They stood in silence side by side. Liz had one hand on the buggy handle and the other held the ferry handrail. Henry's arm hung loosely over her shoulders, the other beside hers on the rail. They were coming into Dymchurch, when Henry had the idea. He turned to her, face suddenly flushed with excitement. "Why don't you come and live at the house?"

Liz looked askance at the farmer, shook his arm off her shoulders, and said, sharply, "What?"

Holding his hands up like a mime, Henry protested and spoke quickly. "No, no. I-I didn't mean—not like that, no. Look, Dick is moving to London soon and this bloke, Simon, is going to move in, help with the farm. Two men on their own, you know, we could do with a housekeeper." He was gabbling and he knew it but couldn't stop. "I could pay you a proper wage, and you could have Dick's flat at the back of the house. It would be good for the kids and good for me to have some young life about the place. It'll change us all. Come on, what do you think?"

Liz didn't answer. She took deep breaths and held them. Henry was being kind. That hurt a little. She didn't cry but slowly released the air from her lungs. The guys were tying up at the dock. She waited, trying to see the future. Henry took hold of the stroller and began to wheel it off the boat. "Come on, Liz, I know a really good café in the town. I'll buy you breakfast."

32

Humiliated by a woman with plaits, Carter had just wanted to get away. He hated the island and all the trouble it had cost him, not to mention the money. Nothing had gone right since the first time he'd set foot on the place. He capitulated because there was nothing else he could do if he still wanted a daughter, and then, with the help of Amber and Simp, a deal was struck. It took a couple of weeks for the exchange to go through.

Before Carter finally left the island with his product, D.C. had cornered him. "I've got something here you may be interested in." He took a small, flat tin box from his shirt pocket. Inside was a slew of powdery crystals. D.C. said, "You should have a look at this. Got this from a mate, just come back from California. Calls it MDMA."

Carter eyed D.C. suspiciously. "Why would I be interested?" Carter had been taken by a bunch of yokels, and he didn't like it; he'd accepted it, but that didn't mean he wanted to be taken again.

D.C. smiled. "Because it's new. Well, it ain't that new, actually." He turned his head slightly away from Carter and looked about as though someone could overhear. "You know the Sharon Tate murders, by the Manson gang? Well, during the police investigation, the house was searched, and among the list of drugs found was grass and coke, speed and this stuff. So I don't know how new it is, but things take time to trickle down to ordinary people, like acid did, do you get me?"

Carter didn't get him. He looked at the stuff in the tin. He didn't like things he didn't understand. It looked unnatural, almost like tiny crumbs of marble or mica or something. Carter sold simple, straightforward drugs—speed, grass, hash—and knew already he didn't want what was being offered but asked the question anyway: "Why would I be interested?"

It was obvious to D.C. "I could introduce you. You'd be in like at the beginning."

Carter thought about his money and about how much people like D.C. had cost him already. He shook his head.

D.C. frowned. "Look, in ten years everybody will be taking this."

Ten years was a lifetime away to Carter; it didn't compute. "Why?" he asked.

D.C. snapped the tin lid shut and put it back into his shirt pocket. "Because it's fucking lovely, that's why."

When all the business was done, the island folk went pretty much back to normal: fruit and veg got picked, cows got milked, eggs got collected. To some it seemed there was a new ambiance, a fresh sense of togetherness among the islanders, but maybe not. To some, the new, all-smiling Henry was a bit hard to adjust to. When he showed his face in the fields or polytunnels, most of the casuals still expected a mouthful, but no, and after a couple of weeks settling in, Simon more or less took over where Dick had left off. He was big but his personality was calm. The workers took easily to him.

After the showdown with the islanders, Carter and his boys were taken back to Dymchurch. Amber went along, not exactly for the ride but to mollify her father and help him come to terms with the loss of his only real friend and a big wodge of money. Amber spent a couple of days with him.

When she went back to Dick, she laughed. "I still don't know what hurt him most, Simp leaving or the money."

Dick moved to London with Amber that weekend. Simon stayed and visited with Henry. They walked the land and talked, and later, over cider and sandwiches, they came to an arrangement. It was easy. Both wanted and needed something other: another way. A few weeks after Dick left, Liz took over his flat at the back of the house and began housekeeping duties for the two men.

Julie and John Newman spent a lot of time together working to set up the co-op with Petal. They claimed it took weeks. Sometimes they worked late and some nights when Petal wasn't even there and Julie didn't go home. Petal nudged her. "Blimey, Mum, now Dad knows, why don't you move in? It's like you're there all the time anyway, and it's a bit weird when you're there and I'm there with Si." She wrinkled her nose.

Julie laughed. "Do I sense an ulterior motive here? Is it possible you're thinking if I moved there, you and Si could—"

Petal clapped her hands and said, disingenuously, "Move into the cottage? You're so clever! What a good idea, I never thought of that."

The vicar and Postmistress P posted their marriage bands. There was a party for that. There were a few parties. Parties because the ferry was saved, because the island folks had pulled off a scam, because new friendships had been made and people like to celebrate. The main one, held in the street outside the post office, had half the island turned up, with barbecue and salads, bread, and soup, and lights like Christmas strung across the street, cake and coffee and cider, and smoke for whoever wanted it and D.C. with his tin of MDMA giving dabs to whoever wanted to give it a go—the kind of party where the islanders, young or old, boogied down to disco music. There was literally dancing in the street.

Later, when it was over, some people went down to the beach and built a fire. Nothing much happened. People lay about and watched the fire, drinking, smoking, chatting. John Newman and D.C. were propped up on their elbows, side by side in the sand, sharing a joint. Across the flames, Petal and Si were cuddled together. Newman nodded across at them. "Look at them, eh? It's good to see them together at last."

D.C. nodded without looking up. His wife and his best mate were moving in together and there was nothing he could say. His daughter and his best mate's son were moving in together and there was nothing he could say. The total inevitability of life did his head in sometimes. It just rolled on regardless.

Newman said, "He's right for her, don't you think?"

Unable to avoid it, D.C. glanced at them, all loved up and wrapped around each other in a big blanket. Petal looked so completely happy. What could he say? What could he do? And what more, as a father, could he ask for? "Your right, mate, and Si is a good man, like his father, but with luck and a fair wind, Petal will manage to keep him off the straight and narrow."

The two men smiled and laughed and shared a shot from the whiskey bottle lying on the grass between them.

Simp was on the beach too, feeling fine and happy, full of good food, good cider, good smoke, and a few dabs of that stuff D.C. had. What did he call it? Whatever. It was good, you couldn't argue with it. Or maybe he was just happy because he'd got a new business and a new life, and also, he wanted to dance but there was no music, and he wanted to hug someone. For no reason he could think of, he stood up and stretched. It felt good. He felt good. Up in the high heavens the stars were twinkling, and the sparks from the fire were rushing up in a swirl of smoke and heat to meet them. Simp felt a sudden rush of joy. He looked about him at the people around the fire. There were no arguments, no rows, no fights, and no power plays, and he knew it wasn't all quite real but it was, for the moment. Standing beside him was Henry Stick, his new partner. He couldn't believe his luck. He turned and opened his big arms wide, encompassed Henry Stick, and hugged him. Henry drew back his head and looked at the big lunk holding him and couldn't find anything to be annoyed about.

Phil Paloney came over and sat beside the fire. Newman passed him the joint and D.C. pulled a plastic bag from his combat jacket pocket. "Still got some of last year's magic mushrooms here. Do you fancy a few?"

Both Paloney and Newman held out their hands: "Why not?"

ABOUT THE AUTHOR

Tim Orchard is a carpenter based in London. *Stickle Island* is his first novel.

@unnamedpress

facebook.com/theunnamedpress

unnamedpress.tumblr.com

www.unnamedpress.com

@unnamedpress